M000312107

STICKY FINGERS 2

JT LAWRENCE

FIRE FINCH

ALSO BY JT LAWRENCE

FICTION

WHEN TOMORROW CALLS
• *SERIES* •

The Stepford Florist: A Novelette (Oct 2017)

The Sigma Surrogate (2018)

1. Why You Were Taken (2015)
2. How We Found You (May 2017)
3. What Have We Done (October 2017)

STANDALONE NOVELS

The Memory of Water (2011)

Grey Magic (2016)

SHORT STORY COLLECTIONS

Sticky Fingers (2016)

Sticky Fingers 2 (2018)

Sticky Fingers 3 (2018)

❧

NON-FICTION

The Underachieving Ovary (2016)

❧

STICKY FINGERS 2

JT LAWRENCE

CONTENTS

1. Panama Wings   1
2. Gatsby's Double   21
3. Astrid   29
4. GlobeTrotter69   46
5. Court, Marry, Kill   62
6. Can We Light a Fire?   80
7. He Did It   89
8. Alpha Lyrae   111
9. Rockabye Baby   119
10. Dasher   137
11. Kakkerlak   173
12. The Brain Bleacher   186

Acknowledgments   201
About the Author   203

1

PANAMA WINGS

"You think he's guilty?" Devil asks.

Robin Susman pulls the key out of the ignition and wrenches the door handle of her bashed-up Honda.

"Yes." She climbs out. "I'm just not sure what of."

They lope to the gate in the shade of the palms, buzz the intercom, and after three beats the metal lock clicks open. Beaulac waits at the front door, dishevelled and scratching his three-day-long stubble.

De Villiers holds up his detective badge, and Beaulac squints into the light, as if he's just come from a dark room.

"I know who you are," he waves away the ID. "They call you Devil."

"Term of endearment," says De Villiers.

"Well," says Beaulac, rubbing the front of his stained T-shirt. "You'd better come in."

The interior of the Beaulacs' expensive security complex home is as knotty as his appearence. Dirty noodle bowls and crushed beer cans litter the otherwise luxurious-looking carpet. Susman hides her annoyance at the banality of it all. No matter how much money they have, she thinks, they always fall apart in the same way. Noodle bowls and beer tins. Oil-stained pizza boxes and empty whisky bottles. She'd seen this picture a thousand times.

"Five days," says Beaulac.

Susman steps closer to the man, her nostrils twitch. There's this picture, and then there are the ones on the other side of the equation: the reason for the distress. The other half. The better half. In this case, she's sure: the worse-off half.

"The last time you saw your wife?"

Beaulac blinks his bleary eyes, clears his throat. "Tuesday, nine a.m."

"Tuesday the 14th of July. And you only reported her missing last night?"

"I didn't realise she was missing."

Little pops go off in Robin's head. Her fingers tingle. She has the urge to wreck the house even more. She needs to keep her anger under control, be professional. She sends her fury into her jaws and grits her teeth.

"You didn't realise she was missing?" Devil's using his pen to lift the edge of a receipt on the flecked black marble of the kitchen island. CURRY DEN, it says. R228.

"I just thought..." He gazes at the floor, but doesn't finish his sentence.

"You thought she left you," says Susman. He looks up at her. "You didn't want to phone the police about your wife leaving you."

"Yes."

"And she travels a lot, you know, for the agency. She could have just forgotten to tell me."

"But then you couldn't get hold of her. Her parents haven't heard from her. Her best friend. She hasn't used any of her bank cards."

"And she didn't take anything with her," Beaulac says, scrubbing his greasy black hair with his knuckles. "She didn't pack a bag. Her passport is still here."

"Her best friend," says Devil. "Do you mean Sasha Noon?"

Noon had also only called them yesterday. Would you wait four days before alerting the police to the disappearance of your closest friend? Would you even know she was missing?

"You've been in contact with Noon?" asks Devil.

"No," says Beaulac. He's lying. He looks at a framed picture on the wall: two schoolgirls in blue uniforms with their arms over each others' shoulders. They could be sisters.

"Funny," says Susman.

"Funny?"

"That you both reported her missing yesterday. You both waited four days. We guessed that maybe you talked."

"No," he says.

De Villiers crosses his arms. He's definitely lying.

Robin snaps on her latex gloves and finds the passport and other clues that Mrs Beaulac—Ursula Beaulac—had not packed up and left her husband. A make-up bag; a pink razor; a full underwear drawer; a brush with plenty of long dark hair tangled up in its bristles.

Susman zips up the razor and hairbrush in a clear plastic bag, pockets it, then pokes around a bit more. In the bin she finds used tissues, a cotton pad smeared with mascara, and an empty, torn box of Femcycle. She looks for the missing pills on the bedside table and in the drawer, but all she finds is a hospital admission bracelet and a Spanish dictionary. They'd be back with a full forensic team to test for blood stains and foreign fingerprints, but she'd have to push for that. The station is understaffed and under-resourced, and she'd have to give a very good reason if she wanted a morning of Luminol and blue light. Usually you'd need a dead body before qualifying for such luxuries.

Beaulac watches her.

"Was your wife on contraception?" she asks him.

He looks shocked by the question, buries his hands in his hair again. It could really do with a wash.

Robin frowns at him. "What? You don't know?"

"No?"

"You were trying for children?"

"No!"

"You used condoms."

Beaulac shakes his head. "What does this have to do with anything?"

4

"Just gathering facts, Mister Beaulac. I've now learnt that you two either weren't having sex, or you weren't close enough to know what kind of birth control she was on."

"*Is* on," says Beaulac. "What birth control she *is on*. She's not dead."

Susman runs the pads of her fingers over the transparent plastic straining against the hard brush bristles in her pocket.

Isn't she? she wants to ask, but doesn't. Best not to push him too far, too soon. There would be a time for that.

"What was that about?" asks Devil when they're back in the sun-bleached Honda. A long time ago it used to be cherry red, now it's more like a tawny rust. Sometimes Robin thinks that is what her heart must look like: faded; corroded; scented with copper.

"Hmm?" Susman's eyebrows arch.

They're on the highway and she forces herself to look out the window, at the sky. The blue is woven through with the white cotton thread of cirrus clouds.

"The 'fact-gathering' bullshit."

"It's not bullshit. Every detail matters."

She licks NikNak crumbs off her fingers and turns the radio on. Crumples the foil packet into a ball and pushes it into the hard pocket of the car door.

Every detail matters, shouldn't the Devil of all people know that?

Susman sees these kinds of details as iron shavings on a board, and the crime is the hidden magnet. Sooner or later, enough of the pieces will point in the right direction. On television series and films there are often substantial clues; the kind that form the turning point of the investigation. And while these are great for entertainment, and they certainly do happen in real cases, in Robin's experience you're not always fortunate enough to catch a break like that. So you need to be clever and cautious with the small things; the things less intuitive cops miss. You owe it to the victim to notice them; to paint the invisible, visible, and in doing so, if you're lucky, you'll paint the victim visible, too.

Robin jabs at the radio dash, trying to find the right channel. "So she didn't pack anything, right? Her passport, her bags, they're all still there."

"Yes," says Devil, eyes on the road. "It's not looking good for the Beaulacs."

"Agreed."

Susman finally finds a station broadcasting the news. "But there was one thing missing."

"Her contraceptive pill," says De Villiers.

"It might be a coincidence. Or a red herring."

A rust-coloured herring?

"But you don't think it is."

"Whenever I pack to go anywhere, before I leave the house…"

The detective laughs. "Since when do *you* go anywhere?"

Robin ignores the jibe. "I never worry about what I've left behind, because things like hairbrushes can easily be replaced.

But I always make sure I have two things: my wallet, and my pill."

The radio show host reads the latest news and plays a few clips of an earlier interview.

"... If found, the E340 debris will furnish clues to events on board before the aircraft crashed. As the search for the missing plane continues, there have been competing theories that it suffered mechanical failure or was intentionally flown off-course. *Boeings don't just go missing,* said South Africa's head of aviation security. *Someone may have deliberately switched off the plane's transponder. We're doing everything we can to support Panama Wings in their investigation.*"

"It's weird, isn't it?" Susman's craving coffee, now. Maybe she'll buy one for Devil. They take their caffeine fix the same way: white, no sugar.

"How does a plane just disappear? A huge capsule of steel and glass flying through the sky just like any other day, and then, crack! It disappears out of existence."

"Not out of existence," says De Villiers. "You heard what he said. Just because we can't find it, doesn't mean it's disappeared."

It's good to have Devil here, to ground her. Sometimes she gets wrapped up in her own head and then the world seems like an incredibly unstable place. She's got enough to deal with, with people living and dying, killing and surviving, without having to think of objects and humans randomly popping in and out of existence.

"We'll only know for certain what happened when we find that black box," says the man on the radio.

"So did she leave him, or is she dead?" wonders Devil aloud.

"Unfortunately those things are not mutually exclusive."

Devil grunts in agreement, and removes a piece of flint from the knee of his navy trousers.

Susman switches off the radio. "I think she's dead."

"Shit."

Devil knows that Susman has a knack for these things. When they first started working together, before the bad things happened to her, before it all fell apart, he learned what she has always known: that she has an otherworldly knack for knowing when someone has died, even if she'd never met them.

They pull up outside a takeaway coffee shop. The car behind them hoots for taking too long to park, and Robin broadcasts her middle finger.

"How do you know?" he asks. "That she's dead?"

"I don't know. It's just a feeling. I could be wrong."

"Ja, well, there's a first time for everything."

Back at the station, Khaya catcalls Susman as she walks in, and she smacks him on the back of the head with the case file she's holding.

"Didn't your mother teach you any manners?" she asks.

"Don't get me started on Khaya's mother," says Blom.

"*Tsek*," says Khaya, and clicks his tongue.

"Stop it, you lot," says De Villiers. "Haven't you got work to do?"

Blom stands up and hands Devil a piece of paper from his— worryingly tidy—desk.

"The report you asked for," he says. "Jane Doe."

The list is short. Only three woman's bodies fitting the description of Ursula Beaulac have been found in the last week. The DNA on the hairbrush Robin brought in will be cross-referenced with the remains, but she can't help looking at the ID shots. All three women have dark hair—same as Ursula—but judging from the teeth and cheekbones, Susman shakes her head.

"Not there?" asks Khaya.

"No point in guessing. Tell the lab to hurry up, will you?"

Khaya brings Robin a sandwich and a mug of grey coffee.

"That missing plane," says Susman. "Can we get a passenger list?"

De Villiers frowns at her. "She wasn't on that plane."

Robin shoots him a look. "Prove it."

"You heard the woman," De Villiers says to Khaya. "Snap snap."

After Khaya leaves, Susman takes a sip of the coffee and pulls a face.

The detective laughs. "Be honest. You've missed being here."

"Um, nope."

"You have."

"I haven't."

"You can't be serious. What do you do all day at that farm, anyway? It's in the middle of bloody nowhere."

"Yes, that's the point. That's why I bought it."

"No, man. You belong here. Can't you feel it?"

"No. I belong in the Free State."

At home is where she can breathe the air and stretch her limbs without feeling like she's bumping into shadows everywhere she turns. Because that's what Joburg is like for her: a forest of elbow-to-elbow ghosts.

"Jesus, Susman. We need you. You may not need us, but it's not the same here without you."

"Well, I need the farm. And the lambs ... they need me."

"The *vokken* sheep? Aren't you as bored as shit out there?"

Devil almost breaks the pencil he is gripping in both hands.

"Never bored. There's a lot to do. I'm up at 4am most mornings to get it all done."

He tosses the pencil onto his bird's nest of a desk and shakes his head. "It's just such a waste," he says. "Such a goddamn waste."

At night, in her Johannesburg hotel, Robin can hear the lambs crying for her in her sleep. It's one of her less terrifying dreams.

"I found something," says Blom, leaning against the doorframe of De Villiers' office.

"That's why you're my favourite," says Robin.

"Hey!" shouts Khaya from his desk next door. "I brought you a sandwich!"

Susman yells back through the chipboard wall. "That sandwich was not fit for human consumption!"

Blom stands on his toes to look over Susman's shoulder and sees in her bin the crumpled ball of wax paper. The sandwich is gone. He smirks.

"Spit it out, Blom," says De Villiers. His cheeks are red; he's still annoyed at Robin for being stubborn.

"Detective Susman asked me to—"

"She's not a detective," says Devil. "Not anymore."

"Sorry," Blom says. "Some habits are hard to break."

"I asked you to check the Beaulac paper trail," says Robin.

"Lots of debt. We're talking mountains, here. She owned a travel agency and it was tanking. And hospital bills," says Blom. "Ursula Beaulac was in ICU in April. I asked for the medical records, but they were cagey."

"Hmm," says Susman.

"Also, there was a new debit order on their joint account," says Blom. "Three months' worth of payments. I traced it to First Lib."

"Ah," says Robin, sitting back in her chair. "Now that *is* interesting."

"Let me guess," says De Villiers. "Mister Beaulac took out insurance on his wife's life."

11

"What an idiot," says Robin. "He may as well have made a bright green neon flashing sign pointing to himself."

"Ten million flashing signs," says Blom, and Devil whistles.

"Good catch," says Susman. "But you don't get the day off. I want you to keep digging. We have a body to find."

❖

De Villiers turns up the volume on the station's TV.

"Hey, breaking news. They found that plane."

There is helicopter and diver footage of the smoky fuselage. Wreckage floating in the ocean. Over two hundred passengers dead. As Robin stares at the screen it feels as if the blue of the sea will seep into her and make her cold forever.

"Fuck," says Susman. "Where's that passenger list?"

Khaya shrugs. "Dead end. Excuse the pun."

"What do you mean?"

"Sorry, that was pretty tasteless. I'll take my foot out of my mouth now."

"No, I mean, why is it a dead end?"

"There was only one South African on the plane. A man."

"I didn't ask you how many South Africans were on the plane. I asked you for a passenger list."

Khaya sighs, and pretends to curtsy. "Yes, madam."

"I love it when you call me that," says Robin, and Blom scoffs.

"I don't know what your obsession is with that plane," says De Villiers. "She didn't take her passport, remember?"

Robin switches off the TV, but it's too late. The cool blue saltwater is in her veins. Her hands start to shake, so she shoves them deep into her pockets.

Of the two hundred and thirty one passengers on the Panama Wings E340 flight, ninety-six were adult women, twenty-eight of whom were around Ursula Beaulac's age. Of those, only one of the bodies was unidentified.

"They couldn't explain it," says Khaya. "They said this body didn't match anyone on the passenger list."

"Hmm," says Susman, biting down on the cheap ballpoint pen in her mouth.

"No way it's her," says Devil. "That's reaching. Even for you, and your magic hunches. Anyway, what does Ursula Beaulac have to do with Panama?"

"Clive Beaulac said she used to travel a lot for work, right?"

"To Panama?"

"She owned a travel agency."

"But her passport didn't have one stamp in it. Not one."

"Okay, that is strange."

"Not strange," says Blom, sauntering in. "My wife does it all the time."

"We don't want to know what your wife does all the time," jokes Khaya, but no one laughs.

"Marguerite has dual citizenship. She travels on her Dutch passport."

"Beaulac doesn't have dual citizenship," says Khaya. "I checked."

"Send them Beaulac's DNA," says Susman.

"You're crazy," says De Villiers.

Khaya looks at him, then Robin, then back at the detective.

"Well?" says Devil. "What are you waiting for?"

"Lab came back with a negative match on the Jane Does," calls Blom.

"Thanks," yells Robin, standing and arching her stiff back. She isn't used to sitting in offices anymore. She does some breathing work, and stretches.

"Can I have some of whatever it is you're smoking?" asks Khaya.

"What?" says Robin. She's distracted, and only half listening. "Are you going to make me another sandwich?"

"The Panama people," he says. "They're on the phone for you."

"Impossible," says De Villiers, but now there is a glint in his eyes.

Susman almost stumbles over the brown box of paperwork in her way. She regains her balance, but not before Devil says: "Smooth."

When she reaches the old telephone she's so keen to hear the voice on the other side she feels like crawling into the receiver.

"We have an odd situation," says the man who doesn't introduce himself. His accent is Rio and roses.

"The DNA matched," Robin says.

"Who is she?" He wants to know. "How did she get on our plane?"

"Is she ... definitely dead?"

"I'm looking at her right now. She's ... definitely dead."

"Can you get someone to send me the passport information of the missing woman? The woman she was supposed to be?"

"I'll do it personally."

"Sasha Noon," says Khaya. "The name in the fake UK passport."

"It's not fake," says Robin.

"Holy shit." De Villiers stands and grabs his jacket. "What is going on here?"

Susman pats her pocket for her car keys. "Let's go pay a visit to Noon."

Beaulac's black SLK is parked outside Sasha Noon's house. As soon as Robin steps out of her car she hears the fighting. Devil raises his eyebrows. Beaulac's voice gets louder, and a woman Robin guesses is Sasha starts to scream at him to leave. Devil presses the button to ring the doorbell. Either it's not working, or the couple ignore the sound. The screaming increases in volume, and then she is quiet, as if her air has been cut off.

"Beaulac!" shouts Susman, rattling the gate. "Beaulac!"

Devil has his Z88 in his hands. Robin didn't even see him reach for it.

"Clive Beaulac!" shouts Robin, her nerves popping.

"He's going to kill her," she says.

The detective pushes her backwards and out of the way, and blows a hole in the lock of the pedestrian gate. The bullet zings and the lock smokes, and they run into the property. Robin's got her gun out now, too, and they barge through the wide front door, looking for Noon.

"Sasha!" she shouts. "Where are you?"

They rush into empty rooms and then into the main bedroom, where Beaulac has his hands wrapped around Sasha Noon's neck, and her eyes are bulging.

Devil holsters his gun and throws himself on Beaulac, hauling him off the woman. Robin aims her 9mm at his chest. "Easy, now," she says.

With one eye on Clive she holds out her hand to Sasha, but she won't get up. She lies there on her white bed and her hands creep up to her throat. She lets out strangled sobs.

Beaulac's also crying, now. "It's your fault!" he yells at her while they both cry.

"Simmer down, Beaulac," says De Villiers.

Sasha says something, but it comes out garbled.

"What's that?" asks Robin. "What are you trying to say?"

She strains to talk; her neck is white and purple and snaked with angry veins.

"He's right," she says, and weeps. "It's my fault she's dead."

Twenty minutes later Sasha Noon is curled up in a dressing gown and sipping tea in the large wingback chair in her open-plan kitchen. Her dark hair is striking against the white robe.

"I can take you to hospital," says Robin.

"It's not necessary," says Noon. "No harm done, not really." Her eyes are still bloodshot from the pressure of Beaulac's hands around her neck.

"No harm done?" says Susman. The sooner she sees Beaulac in prison, the better. Devil was busy interrogating him outside, in the garden. At least they have a reason to arrest him, now.

"I mean ... I'm still alive."

Her implication hangs in the air.

"Why did you say that it's your fault Ursula's dead?"

Her face crumples, and Susman thinks she's going to cry again, but she doesn't.

"They always said we looked like sisters," Sasha says. "Since school. Did you know we went to school together?"

"No," says Susman, but then she remembers the photograph of the two girls in blue uniform, a white school crest on their hats.

"They used to mix up our names. We used to play along. We swapped clothes and cut our hair in the same style. Twins, they used to say. Even our parents."

"So Ursula used your UK ID to book that flight to Panama."

"Yes."

"You gave her your passport and your bank cards."

"It wasn't the first time. We had a few trial runs, first, to make sure we could pull it off."

"She used it for her work trips?"

"Yes," says Sasha. "Nobody blinked an eyelid."

"Why did you do it? Was it just a game?"

"No, it was part of our plan. We had everything planned. It took months to organise."

"Your plan?"

"To help Ursula disappear."

Sasha blinks away the persistent tears, then wipes her wet cheeks on the sleeve of her robe. She sniffs, and pulls herself together.

"Clive was abusive to her?" Robin asks.

"No," Sasha shakes her head. "No, nothing like that. But their marriage was over, and he was clinging to it. She didn't have the energy for the fight, or the money for a divorce. Her business had been struggling, she was in debt. A lot of debt. She kept on applying for more and more credit but the banks had started to refuse her. She just felt like ... like she wouldn't ever be able to get out of the hole she in. That's how she described it. A giant hole that she couldn't imagine climbing out of."

"Was she depressed?" asks Robin.

"More than that. One night she phoned me at two in the morning and she was just crying, hysterical, said she couldn't do it anymore."

"Do what?"

"She'd bought pills, a whole lot of pills. And a bottle of gin. She was phoning to say goodbye."

"You took her to hospital."

"They pumped her stomach. Two nights in ICU. When Clive found out, he lost it. It made things even worse. I knew she would try to commit suicide again, so we came up with a plan together, to give her a brand new life."

"In Panama."

"She knew the area, had done some consulting for a hotel group. She even spoke a little Spanish. She was supposed to live in a small village in Boquete, surrounded by coffee plantations and green hills. Start over, you know? But then—"

"But then the plane crashed."

If Devil had been in this conversation, he'd say: *and then the* vokken *plane crashed.*

Sasha's fingers find their way back to her bruised neck over and over again.

"It's so crazy. So surreal. I feel like I'm dreaming. I can't believe she's dead. This was supposed to save her life."

"I'm sorry for your loss," says Robin.

"She *is* dead, right? I mean, she didn't pull a little last-minute plot twist and get on another plane altogether?"

"Unfortunately not. The DNA match was conclusive. They'll repatriate the body to the South African authorities."

Sasha gets a faraway look in her eyes. She doesn't want to listen to talk of bodies, not when it's her dearest friend they're discussing.

"She did say it would be too good to be true. When we fanta-sised about what her new life would be like, there. She said she'd get some chickens and live off pancakes, and the fruit trees on the property. I joked that she'd meet a handsome local and have little sun-bronzed Panama babies."

Sasha smiles, luxuriating in the day-dream. Robin thinks of her own paradise, her lonely farm, and is relieved she'll be able to return soon. She misses the warmth and the scent of the lambs, the red soil, the gold shimmers in the air as the sun sinks down.

The dream evaporates and Sasha sniffs again, holds her neck. "It was supposed to save her life."

～

2

GATSBY'S DOUBLE

It starts with a dog's bark.

I flinch, and look up from my work: smears of bright oil paint on the linen canvas I stretch myself. I'm busy with a nude, but I'm best at portraits. The studio smells of turpentine and hot wax. The fumes may cause others' noses to tingle, but I'm most at home with this piney, petrol smell. Younger artists say that turps isn't good for your lungs. They might be right, but I'm an old dog, and there's a limit to how many new tricks I'm willing to learn.

I hear the bark again, as if the hound has read my thoughts, and agrees. This makes me feel restless. I toss my brush into the wide-mouthed jar of cobalt violet solvent—an old mayonnaise jar, perhaps, or gherkins with dill—and stand up, wiping paint off my fingers and palms with the pungent cloth I keep nearby. I leave my apron on. I am most comfortable in my apron, and I plan to come right back to continue my work. But that bark ... there is something odd in that bark.

I kick the bottom of the studio door to open it (it's an old, swollen door, and it has a well-worn brass doorknob which I love to touch). The glass panels are clear but textured, so when someone stands behind it, his face is transformed into a pointillist painting. One day my kick will dislodge a pane of glass and it will no doubt shatter, or fall and stab one or both of my perennially bare feet.

The scuffed parquet floor is cool under my soles. Burnt Sienna; Indian Red; Naples Yellow. The air in the passage is always chilled, dark and stagnant compared to my studio which is bleached by sunlight and fresh air. I'm used to the corridor's dimness and it does not bother me on a normal day. On the contrary, it makes for a welcome relief after hours of painting in the bright light. But today is not a normal day.

The passage leads to the kitchen, and the sitting room. To the left is the guest toilet. I've lived here for forty years. I could draw a map for you, blindfolded and sitting on a horse.

The dog yaps again, and I freeze. Where *is* the little tyrant? I force myself to keep going, despite the sense of foreboding I feel boiling in my intestines. I step into the kitchen and see him: a grey Pomeranian so fluffy you'd think I put him in the tumble dryer (I don't). He stares at me with his shiny black marbles, his fur is an electric shock. A slight pant; a salmon-pink tongue. Who is this creature?

"Who are you?" I say to the dog.

He looks exactly like Gatsby, but he's not. I should know. I've had Gatsby for sixteen years and a man knows his dog. I could pick Gatsby out from a line-up a hundred meters away. I know my Gatsby.

"Yes?" I say, "Who are you? Where did you come from?"

The dog yaps and keeps staring at me. I stare back.

Did Gatsby somehow smuggle this dog in from the park, so that he'd have someone to play with? I haven't been very good at replacing his toys recently. Perhaps he was bored.

"Gatsby?" I call. The dog in front of me barks and wags his tail. "Gatsby?"

I amble around the house, looking in all of his favourite lounging places. The bed in the laundry room, the footrest in the lounge, the old viridian beanbag near the television in my bedroom. The little dog follows me from room to room.

"Gatsby?" I call again, and whistle. "Here boy, here boy, come here boy."

The other dog barks and jumps up onto his back legs. That's a Gatsby trick. I wonder if Gatsby taught him how to do that.

I fetch a bone-shaped dog biscuit from the tin and in the kitchen and whistle my special Gatsby whistle, but still no sign of my little grey Pom. I wonder if someone is playing a trick on me. If I had a son, or a brother, perhaps they would have stumbled upon a dog that looked to them exactly like Gatsby and decided to play a trick on me.

The imposter walks on his hind legs again, angling for the treat he knows I have in my hand. I can't give it to him. Gatsby would see that as a betrayal. I put the biscuit back into the tin and dust the meat-scented crumbs from my hands. The dog bleats a soft whine and scurries over to Gatsby's bed, turning around in a circle till he finds the right place to lie, then closes his eyes and pretends to sleep.

❖

I switch on the kettle, and scratch for an un-chipped mug in the cupboard. I should really get rid of the broken ones, but I've never been good at throwing things away. When I can't find a flawless mug, I impatiently grab the first one in my line of vision. A spiderweb crack runs from the handle to the base. It's too small, and the lip is not my favourite shape, but it will do. I abandon the rushing, steaming kettle and reach instead for my brandy. It would be a little early to drink on a normal day, but today is not a normal day.

I slosh amber liquid into the mug and leave the bottle on the counter, uncapped. I taste caramel and peaches, and the warmth coats the cold sense of dread in my heart. I drink it down and pour myself another one, which I plan to take back to the studio with me, but then I see the canine imposter feigning a nap on Gatsby's bed and I am filled with a deep and stark feeling that not even the brandy can appease.

In my bathroom I approach the fully-stocked medicine cabinet and close the mirrored door. I gasp and drop my mug and it smashes all over the varnished concrete floor. There, staring back at me, is a complete stranger, wearing my clothes, and my paint-splattered apron. My thoughts spin in my head, forming a whirlpool, a vacuum, a black hole. The man, himself shocked, stares back at me with mad, voltaic eyes.

I know better than to ask *Who are you?* this time so I stand there among the sharp ceramic shards and wait. Perhaps he will talk first.

I wait and wait, never breaking eye contact with the strange, slipstream man. At last I cannot stand it anymore. "What are you doing in my bathroom?" I ask. "What are you doing in my mirror?"

The man moves his lips as if he is parroting me, but no sound comes out. The cheek of him! He's pretending to be my reflection. Does he not know that I would know the difference between my own face and a stranger's? I start to get angry, really angry at what is happening. First, they take my dog, then they put a rogue in the mirror.

I get so furious that I want to smash the glass, I want to pull the trickster out and wring his neck.

"Listen," I say to him. "I've had just about enough of this."

The man's eyes glint and burn into mine like hot diamonds. It takes my breath away and I step back. A spoke of pain shears its way through the bottom of my foot and I cry out. The man looks sorry, so my heart softens against him. He can't be that bad, if he has that reaction when someone hurts himself. No, he probably has a great deal of empathy, and, let me tell you, empathy is hard to come by these days. Perhaps we'll talk and become friends. Perhaps he'll be here for me every day, and I'll greet him every morning while I bungle through my morning toiletry routine.

Perhaps we just started out on the wrong foot, I think, my own foot glowing with pain as it dyes the floor Perylene Red. So I start to talk to him, the man in my medicine cabinet mirror, and I'm pleased when his face relaxes and he angles his head to better hear my stories. He listens for a very long time, until I get faint from hunger, so I stop for a moment and ask him to wait.

I run downstairs (cochineal footprints) and grab a plate of food from the fridge, and a fork. On second thoughts, I get two sets of cutlery, in case the man is hungry, too.

When the light in the bathroom begins to turn grey, and my throat is sore from talking, I hear a click and a shuffle from downstairs.

"I'm up here!" I yell.

I hear her steady footsteps as she climbs the stairs, and I turn to greet her, but her face turns the colour of an ivory piano key. Her handbag drops to the carpet, and I wonder how many things are broken every day by people who get little shocks like these, like white currents in your fingers.

"I know what you're thinking," I say. She's also frightened by the phoney in the mirror, but I'm going to tell her he's okay. He's actually quite nice, when you get to know him, but before I have time to say anything she cuts me off with a voice like a tightrope.

"Richard," she says, "what has happened?"

I frown, and look down, and I see that the bathroom floor is painted red with blood.

"I cut my foot," I say.

Lori rushes towards me, but hesitates at the blackened edge of the puddle. A darkening gradient of crimson to umber.

"Come to me," she says, "can you walk?"

I bend my knee and pull the injured foot up to get a better look at it. Lori gasps. A ceramic dagger juts out of the delicate sole-skin like a shark's fin. I get a good grip on it and yank it out, and Lori yells as more blood spurts out. The wound is deep and wide, like a canyon, and it makes me think of men who get stuck in canyons and have to cut their limbs off to escape.

"Do you think I'll lose my leg?" I ask Lori, who looks like she's about to faint.

"No," she says, shaking her head, blinking away her lightheadedness, "You're not going to lose your leg."

We stumble down the stairs together, and I try not to lean on Lori too much. She's a petite woman, and I've always tried to protect her from my inelegant, bulky frame. *More like a rugby player than an artist,* my father used to say, but he didn't actually mind that I took to the arts more than the field.

Gatsby senses the excitement and starts barking, and rushes over to us as we reach the bottom of the stairs. I'm so relieved that he's back, and I'm about to say so when I see the dog and realise it's not Gatsby at all, but the little hoaxer with the puffed out ash-coloured fur. He has learnt to bark like Gatsby, which fills me with a virulent panic that splashes orange into my veins. It makes me think of orpiment, the arsenic-rich volcanic mineral used as a pigment for centuries despite its noxious malice. Heat transforms it from a mellow yellow to a vivid, glowing orange—oxygen on a hot coal—and that is how my insides feel.

Lori leads me to my chair and pulls up the foot stool—the leather one, ball and claw—and throws a ragged towel over it, then places my foot gently on top. Her cool fingers are balm for my throbbing sole, and I feel so much gratitude and fondness for her in that moment, but then the horrible hound yaps and the illusion is shattered. I look at the woman fussing with the first aid kit, tearing plasters and uncapping foul-smelling green antiseptic, and I realise that it's not Lori at all.

The woman looks like my wife, and is wearing my wife's clothing, but it's certainly not Lori. The fraudsters would get away with this kind of thing, but they didn't count on my gut, because, emotionally speaking, the Lori kneeling at my feet is like a black-and-white photocopy. She's got all the right bits in all the right places, but her essence is missing. Her core. How do you explain that to someone who has never had to deal with this kind of thing? They've taken Lori and Gatsby and left me with these animated but empty shells.

Where is Lori? What do I do? Maybe if I grab a knife from the kitchen and hold it against her neck she'll tell me where my real wife is. The coal burns and burns.

"Did you take your pills today?" the clone asks. "If you're not feeling very well, it might be because you forgot to take your pills."

I think of the brimming medicine cabinet lined with little bottles of tablets in varying tints of blue. Cyan, Sky, Indigo, Cobalt, Sapphire. Did I take my pills this morning? I can't remember. I think I must take my pills to feel better, but then a different thought strikes me like a bolt of fiery lightning. What if the pills are made by the imposters? What if they are drugging me so that I don't notice when they take everyone from me and replace them with soulless replicas? In fact, isn't that why I didn't take them this morning? I look at Gatsby, who is staring at me again with his shiny black marbles and quivering fur. I look at Lori, who frowns as she wraps my foot in a clean white bandage. A hot shiver spikes my spine.

I make a mental note to never take the pills again.

~

3

ASTRID

THE NEW PRESCHOOL was so beautiful and so sweet. To be completely honest, I probably would have enrolled Astrid even if it hadn't been. I had arrived at the introductory meeting ready to sign the enrolment form before seeing the inside or meeting the teachers, because there was no other preschool in the area and I desperately needed one for my three-year-old daughter. The fact that it was located on a nice, quiet street within walking distance of our house was an added bonus. Despite being brand new, the school was filling up quickly and I needed to get Astrid placed before it was too late.

On my way to the twenty-minute tour—booked online—I remember feeling guilty, because I had a feeling that nothing short of the teachers being actual werewolves would stop me from signing that form.

But then I arrived and fell in love, and the guilt evaporated. The sweetest garden was planted outside the front gate: irises—which just happen to be my favourite flowers—and small daisies and soft grasses and fairy cups and timber toadstools painted cherry and white. The roof was sky blue, the front door London

Bus red (the same as ours at home) and there was a little white picket fence tucked safely beyond the secure exterior wall. Best of all, there was a swing hanging from a tree. Astrid loves our swing at home.

"This is where they eat their snacks," said Mrs Dalton, her open palm gesturing in the direction of miniature tables and chairs in the front garden, under an old oak tree. It looked like a little al fresco café, with its friendly décor and dappled shade.

"We offer vegan, vegetarian, halaal, kosher, and whole meal programmes. They're fresh, organic, and healthy, with plenty of variety, so you don't have to worry about packing snacks every morning."

"Where do I sign?" I joked, and Mrs Dalton smiled at me. She was an attractive woman, with startling green eyes and a matronly figure. I felt quite bony next to her, and not at all maternal. But this feeling isn't new. I've always felt more comfortable in a room of suits than at a jammy-mouthed toddler's party.

If I was sold on the school before the tour, I was practically trying to throw my money at Dalton afterwards. The furnishing was rather minimalist and stylish for a preschool; what I'd expect a Scandinavian kindergarten to look like. And I *love* Swedish interior design. My husband calls it 'fold-up design' in a deprecating kind of way, and jokes that you must be able to pack up a Swedish house in half an hour if you wanted to; says Ikea's got a lot to answer for. Richard is a little more traditional in his taste. He prefers solid wood, heavy throws, oriental carpets, and bookshelves packed tightly by his out-of-control book collecting habit; while I love white space, clean lines, pale polished timber, and fresh colours.

I thought it was beautiful, and I was sure Astrid would feel the same way. There were little fun touches through-out, like Dr Seuss posters, a spring-to tent shaped like a princess turret, and playful ring-shaped plush pillows that looked like giant straw-berry- and chocolate-glazed doughnuts with rainbow sprinkles.

Some of the rooms were bare. "We're still getting set up," Mrs Dalton said.

"Of course," I nodded. "These things take time."

At sixteen minutes into the tour, we said goodbye at the gate, while Talmon, the security guard, unlocked it for me.

"I'll email you the completed enrolment form tonight," I said.

"Oh, there's no rush, Rebecca," Mrs Dalton said. "We'll keep a place for your Astrid, if you want her to attend here. Why don't you give it a think. Sleep on it. We'll still be here in the morning."

Astrid's first day of school went really well. She wore her favourite dress—white with giant gold polka dots — and said she loved the swing and the plush doughnuts, just like I knew she would. She came home with her plastic apron splattered with crimson and maroon acrylic paint; her hands were tinted blue and perfumed by play dough.

"Do you like your new school?" I asked her on our walk back. She didn't answer, and I didn't want to push it. I was sure she'd take a little while to settle in, as all kids do.

Sometimes, when I arrived to collect her, I would stand at the front gate and observe them for a while, unseen. It looked like Mrs Dalton was very good with the kids, very warm. It was obvious that she and Astrid were forming a close relationship, and I was happy about that.

"A home away from home," the teacher had said to me on my first visit.

After a few weeks, Astrid called Mrs Dalton 'mommy' by mistake while I was dropping her off. We both laughed and brushed it off as completely normal. But a few days later I realised it hadn't been a mistake ... Astrid was calling her 'mommy' all the time.

I didn't like it—it gave me a strange, sick feeling in my stomach—but I decided to not make a big deal about it. It was a positive sign, surely, that she felt so comfortable with Mrs Dalton that she called her that? I mean, she spends so much more time with her than she does with me. I know I work too hard. The hours are long and the work itself is demanding. Poor Astrid is the first one to be dropped off in the morning and the last one to leave. Some days I feel like we don't talk at all.

Mrs D gives Astrid a big hug when it's time to say goodbye in the afternoons.

"She's a very special girl," she always says to me, her green eyes blazing with affection.

"Do you have any friends?" I asked Astrid on one of our walks home. She shook her head. Before, when I had asked her, she said she was lonely at the new school. *There's no one to play with*, she had said. "Just be yourself," I told her. "Smile and be kind. You'll find a special friend soon enough."

One day I arrived twenty minutes late and all the other kids had, as usual, already been collected. The sun was beginning to set, and the outside playground was dimmed to monochrome and empty, which made me shiver. Empty playgrounds give me the creeps. Talmon let me in—I don't think the security guard liked me much, I don't know why—and as I walked down the passage, looking for her, I noticed that some of the rooms were still bare.

"Astrid?" I called. "Mrs Dalton?" and then I was immediately sorry I had called so loudly because there they were, the two of them, curled up on the nap stretcher in the snooze room, fast asleep. Astrid's chubby limbs were virtually glued to Mrs Dalton's, cuddling as only a three-year-old can: octopus-like, but with sweet-smelling, warm skin. They were both sleeping so deeply I couldn't hear them breathe.

I stood and watched them for a moment, lamenting the fact that Astrid had grown so quickly.

Where had my baby gone?

I may not be the most maternal woman ever born, but I did miss those times my milk-fragrant baby would hold fast onto one of my fingers and fall asleep in my arms, and I would get lost in breathing in her pale skin and her soft hair, as the knowledge that those days would soon be over tugged at my heart.

Standing there, I suddenly had the urge to page through her baby book and be reminded of her first tooth, her first steps. I wanted to trace the arc of the snippet of her blonde hair. I only ever look at the first half of the book; the last few pages always make me sad, so I never page past the middle.

My head started aching, and I felt very tearful suddenly, and ridiculous. I blinked away the nostalgia and dried my cheeks.

Mrs Dalton would think I was a mad woman, frozen there watching them sleep, and weeping. My embarrassment didn't erode my heartache, which still burned my chest as I leaned over to softly rouse Astrid.

The poignancy of that moment stayed with me for days afterwards, and I found I was daydreaming of Astrid when I should have been working. While she was at school I caught myself sitting on the heart-patterned quilt on her bed, in her room, my face buried in her blue cuddle bunny, trying to find her smell. I felt this strong urge to hug her, and had the idea that if I could just smell her, it would alleviate the craving. I had already tried her wardrobe, specifically looking for her white and gold dress, but it wasn't there. I tried to find her in the scent of the clothes but they were fragranced with washing powder and sunshine, and in that moment it seemed to me that we were transported outside, and she was standing on the other side of white linen sheets drying on the line, being hidden and revealed as the wind whipped the fabric, just out of reach.

"Do you enjoy the food at school?" I asked Astrid one morning, and she nodded. The school meal programme catered for breakfast, lunch, and an early dinner, plus snacks in between, so I no longer prepared any food for her. It gave me an uneasy feeling. I used to be her only source of nutrition, and now I wouldn't be able to tell you what she had for lunch yesterday. There were still boxes of her snacks in the kitchen cupboard, but they never seemed to need replenishing.

I made her some toast soldiers, glistening with melted butter, and served them on her favourite pink princess plate, kissing her little poppet head as I did so.

When I returned home from dropping her off at school, I flicked on the kettle to make some tea, and noticed the plastic plate was still on the counter. The toast was untouched, and the butter was cold and congealed.

Last night I had the most frightening dream. I still haven't been able to shake it. It's as if I'd been having this slow creep of dread and then my subconscious latched onto it and created the most terrifying nightmare. I woke up screaming and hyperventilating and Richard looked quite pale when he turned on the lights.

Caught between the walls of sleep and consciousness, I imagined he had blood splattered over his face, and I scrambled away from him and screamed louder.

"Rebecca," he said, reaching a hand out for me, which I batted away. "Rebecca! Wake up! You're dreaming!" and then the room started to fall into focus and Richard's face was there again, crumpled by sleep and concern, but clean of blood.

My head was throbbing with pain. He ran me a bath, added some chamomile teabags, and stripped my sweat-soaked pajamas off my shivering body. He sat in the bathroom, watching me soak. He didn't ask for details although I could tell he was anxious. I wanted to tell him to not worry, that it was just a nightmare. But the truth was that something about it, something real, had gripped my heart and had not yet let go.

Astrid had been calling me, in the dream. I couldn't see her, but was trying to find her by following her voice. Is it because I feel we are growing apart? Then I realised we were at her school, but it was virtually unrecognisable because it was now an abandoned building. Doors creaked as they fell off their hinges, and window panes lay shattered on the floor.

"It's lonely here," said Astrid. "There's no colour."

I pictured her in her white and gold dress: torn, dirty, monochrome.

"I'm coming to find you!" I told her.

"I'm so cold," she said. "I'm shivering."

"I'm here with you. I'm going to find you."

But the black-and-white passages just went on forever, revealing more deserted rooms at every turn, and even though I ran and ran, I couldn't find Astrid.

After the bath Richard towelled me off and dressed me in clean pyjamas. We lay together, close, and it was so comforting to just relax and be held. How long had it been that we had lain like this?

"It's going to be okay," he said, rubbing the back of my neck where he knows it still gets sore. "It's going to be okay."

My head kept pulsing against the pillow.

Richard knew not to switch the lights off.

"I think I know what triggered the nightmare," I said the next morning, as we were dressing for work. I applied lipstick and mascara, and made a note to buy more foundation. I seemed to be going through it at a rate.

Richard glanced at me. "Are you going to wear that?"

I looked down. I was wearing charcoal slacks and a silk blouse, with a pin-striped blazer over it. It was one of my go-to corporate suits: stylish and professional.

"What?" I said. "Why?"

He was about to say something, but then thought better of it. I was confused. He used to compliment me when I wore this outfit.

"Tell me," I said. "I want to know. Don't I look good in it anymore?"

He walked towards me and hugged me. "Of course you do," he said, but the suit felt uncomfortable on me for the rest of the day.

❖

"You said you had an idea as to what triggered the bad dream," Richard said at dinner that night, when Astrid was asleep.

"Oh, yes," I said. "I think maybe it was a stress dream, you know?"

Richard's gaze was even. "It is a stressful time," he said.

"I've just been under so much pressure at work, and with Astrid starting school for the first time—"

He broke eye contact with me and pushed his knife and fork

together on his plate, despite having only eaten half of his bolognese.

"Not hungry?" I asked.

He stood up and poured himself a large vodka. "Not anymore."

I was pushing the swing under the tree in our back garden when something occurred to me with a shock. I had been so giddy at the prospect of the school being so convenient and so lovely-looking that I hadn't checked on any of the formal requirements. Was it zoned correctly? Did it have the necessary license? Was Mrs Dalton a qualified preschool teacher? Was that what the dream was trying to tell me?

My neglect socked me in the stomach. I was quite certain everything would be in place when I checked, but the fact that it was only occurring to me now made me feel terrible.

I was busy with work, I told myself. *It's normal for some small things to fall through the cracks.*

But the guilt remained, like great black talons in my shoulders. I knew this was no small thing.

While I continued pushing the swing with my left hand, I unlocked my phone with my right, and found my latest email correspondence with Mrs Samantha Dalton. Under her name and designation were all the right letters: B. Ed. FP. The school also had a registration number.

I began to cross-check the details of her email signature against the department of education's roll, and the school wasn't listed there. Dread dripped like tar in my stomach as I scrolled and scrolled. It definitely wasn't there. Then I remembered that it's a new school, and a new year, and perhaps the roll simply hadn't been updated yet.

Suddenly Richard was beside me and I flinched; I hadn't heard him approach. He took my hand and kissed it.

"You're pushing the swing," he said.

I looked at him as if to say: *Yes. And?* But then I realised the swing was empty.

"I'm worried," I said. "Astrid's school. I can't find it on the school directory. They've got a license number but the school is not in the directory."

Richard rubs his face. "Rebecca."

"Don't you think that's odd? What? Am I just being paranoid?"

"Rebecca," he said again. "Don't do this."

"Do what?"

"You know. You know what you can be like."

I know. I do know. I can be obsessive.

So I kept quiet, and let him lead me inside the house for a cup of tea. But I was determined to get to the bottom of it.

After Richard left for work, I opened up my laptop and searched for Samantha Dalton. Even if the school was new and not yet listed, were her teacher credentials up to date? I searched for her name as my nerves stripped my insides bare. I started shaking so much I was battling to type, and my fingertips were slick with perspiration. I looked again and again, sure I was missing a simple part of the equation, and then I found an

39

article about her and the knowledge came rushing at me like a freight train.

Samantha Dalton had no teaching credentials. Samantha Dalton had no social media profile. Because Samantha Dalton was dead.

Fear flushed my whole body from head to toe, and my heart was almost beating out of my chest.

She had been dead for over a year.

So who was the woman at the school? I pictured her lying with Astrid that day, sleeping so soundly I could not hear them breathing. I pictured her calling my daughter, and Astrid running to her and holding her hand, ready to go anywhere she'd lead her.

I jumped up, knocking over my chair, and ran to get my car keys. They weren't on the key hook. I yelped and swore as I turned my handbag upside down on the kitchen counter. No keys. I didn't have time to search. I had to run there.

When I arrived at the school, sweating and bright red with exertion and jangling nerves, Talmon looked at me with his usual suspicion. He didn't reach for his keys.

"Let me in!" I shouted at him. My head felt like it was going to explode.

"Please, Mrs Robertson, calm down."

"Calm down?" I screeched. "*Calm down?*"

"Let me call Mr Robertson," he suggested. "He can come get you."

"Talmon," I said through gritted teeth. "If you don't let me in I will break down that door."

He started to look uneasy.

"Do you think I'm bluffing?" I demanded. I took a few steps back and steeled myself. This was going to hurt, but I didn't give a toss. I was going to get in there and get my little girl if it killed me.

"Wait," he said, "Wait." And then he clipped his keys off his belt and unlocked the door.

I rushed past him and into the school property, and what I saw made me lose my balance. I fell hard on the fine gravel path, skinning my knees, but I didn't feel the pain. Talmon came to help me up, but I screamed at him to get away. The sky seemed to be swirling, and I tried to ignore it, along with the rushing sound in my ears as I ran inside. The café was gone, the swing. The whole playground was gone. Inside not a puzzle nor poster remained. I started to hyperventilate.

"Astrid!" I screamed. "Astrid!" and I checked all the rooms for her small, sleeping body, but, like in my dream, all the rooms were bare.

I couldn't control my breathing. Panic was squeezing my heart and the feeling of dread was so intense that I fell to the floor. I thought I may be having a heart attack.

Talmon appeared at the door, and slipped his phone into his pocket. "Mrs Robertson. Let me help you."

"They took her," I cried. "Where is she?"

"Mrs Robertson."

I leapt up and flung myself at the guard. I gritted my teeth and flailed at him, punching him over and over in the chest. I scratched and clawed at him like a feral cat.

"Where is she? Tell me where she is!" I shouted over and over again.

I would kill him, I thought, I would kill him if he didn't tell me where to find her.

My mind churned like the heavens outside, pictures and memories and half-formed thoughts. I couldn't make sense of any of them.

Talmon let me lean against him, exhausted, his uniform shirtfront wet from my tears. When I stumbled, he leaned down and hoisted me up, one arm underneath my shoulders, the other underneath my knees, and carried me like a child to the car waiting outside. He laid me in the back seat and pulled the skirt of my dress down to cover my legs.

"Thank you, Talmon," Richard said. "I'm really sorry—"

But I didn't hear the rest of the conversation.

When I woke up at home, on the couch in the lounge, I immediately rushed to Astrid's room. Richard was sitting on her bed, but Astrid wasn't there.

It must have been a dream, I thought. A nightmare about an elaborate kidnapping plan. There was relief, but also fear, because Richard looked calm, but Astrid wasn't there. I thought I might vomit.

"Where is she?" I asked, and the words sounded strange because my mouth was so dry that my tongue was hardly working. Richard patted the quilt next to him.

"Come sit with me," he said. His voice also sounded strange, as if he had been crying.

"Has something happened?" I asked. I felt the panic clawing up again and inside I was shrieking—

Oh God has something happened to Astrid?

And the rushing and swirling thoughts came back and Richard grabbed me and propped me up on our little girl's bed. He had the baby book on his lap.

"The school took her?" I said. "Kidnapped? Police?" I no longer saw the point of using full sentences.

Richard shook his head. "There is no school."

I swallowed hard. "Not anymore?"

"There's never been a school. You made up the school. It was your way of coping with Astrid not being with us anymore. It makes you feel better. When you miss her, when you come in here and—" he broke off, tears in his eyes, "—and she's not here, you tell yourself she's at school."

"No," I said. "The school is real. I go there every day before work."

"Rebecca. You haven't worked in over a year."

"But Mrs Dalton. The fold-up furniture."

"There's no fold-up furniture."

"Mrs Dalton?"

"Samantha Dalton is the woman who—"

"She's real?"

Richard takes my hand. "Samantha Dalton was the woman in the other car."

I blinked at him.

The other car?

I've heard this before.

It all feels familiar but I can't think of what comes next.

This morning I couldn't find my car keys.

Then I remembered that I no longer had a car. I didn't ever want to drive again, after what happened.

"What happened?" I ask, talking past the hot stone in my throat.

Richard frowns. "We made a book," he says, gently touching the cover.

"I know," I said. "I know that book."

"We pasted in some things at the back, to help you remember."

What things? What things? I wanted to know, but I was terrified.

Richard opened the baby book towards the end, and passed it to me. There was a small newspaper article on the left hand side, and a picture of Astrid on the right, wearing her favourite white and gold polka dot dress. It's such a beautiful picture of her.

The newspaper headline said *Highway Collision Claims Two Lives.*

My brain clattered and chimed.

Richard spoke in the most tender voice. "You were in ICU for weeks."

"What?"

I remembered being in bed in a cream-coloured room. There were flowers—irises—and a box of pink doughnuts on the table.

"Massive head trauma." He ran his fingers over the scar I had on my forehead. The one I covered up with make-up every day. "You're still healing."

My heart was pounding so hard I heard it in the walls.

"But you survived," he said, squeezing my hands. "You survived."

I looked at his face, wrecked by emotion, then at the picture of Astrid. It had a date printed beneath it. 2014 - 2017.

I felt like I was being electrocuted from the inside. I grabbed my stomach and doubled over. "No," I said. "No."

But deep down, I knew that it was true.

GLOBETROTTER69

TRIP ADVISOR REVIEW: Twin Palms Resort. 5 out of 5 stars.

I had the good fortune of staying at 'The Twin Palms Resort' in the Eastern Cape, from the 5th till the 12th of October, 2017. Before I go any further I'd like to note that it was rather difficult to secure a reservation, so my advice is to book ahead of time to avoid disappointment!

'The Twin Palms Resort' is a marvellous destination, located just the right distance away from the ocean. It's a short walk to the beach, but the ocean is not so close that you're pestered by sea-spray or joggers or barking crotch-sniffers, or those awful gulls that insist on squawking and squealing as they wheel overhead.

While we're on the subject of the beach, I must say that it's a charming strip, with just the right balance of private and public space. The modest café there serves excellent beer-battered fish and chips, their ice-cream is delicious, and, at the risk of sounding like a sentimental old fool, it made me feel quite nostalgic for my childhood days, when I would walk on the sun-baked sand with ice-cream melting down my chin, holding hands with my beloved Aunt Daphne.

The food at the resort was also wonderful, if a bit salty for my taste. The soups were especially delicious, and I loved the moist, just-baked bread, the room-temperature butter, the fresh salad buffet bar, and the vibrant 'Cultural' evening where the guests were encouraged to join in with the traditional dancing and singing. An excellent time was had by all!

Here are the other things I appreciated about the resort: the extremely comfortable beds (I slept like a baby!), the air conditioning, the housekeeping girl, and the complimentary drinks in the bar fridge.

Suffice to say I thought the resort was top notch. I really did have a wonderful time at 'The Twin Palms Resort' and I am indeed looking forward to my next stay.

Morgan Belafry, AKA @GlobeTrotter69

Dear Globe Trotter

Thank you kindly for your wonderful review. We are so happy that you enjoyed your stay at the Twin Palms.

On the matter of the delay in your reservation: the reason your booking took a long time to finalise is because there was a small issue with your credit card. Bookings are only confirmed on the payment of the initial deposit. When we received the funds, your room was booked without delay.

Thank you again for your kind review, it is much appreciated.

Regards

Vuleka Dandala, Manager, The Twin Palms Resort

∿

Trip Advisor Review: Twin Palms Resort. 4 out of 5 stars.

Dear Ms Dandala

Thank you for your response! Not every hotel takes the time to respond to my reviews and I do so appreciate it when they do. That said, it did make me remember some of the less than stellar aspects of my stay there, so I thought I should make a note of them here for your benefit as well as potential guests reading this.

I have two minor complaints about the beach, for which I docked half a star each. The ocean was just too cold, and too rough. In my mind, a warm, calm sea is like the arms of a lover, and you should be confident to waltz into them and feel welcome and safe. But this swimming spot—despite it being October—I found quite cold and hostile. One only had to be knee-deep before one's toes turned to blocks of ice, and the waves kept beating against me and once even threatened to pull me under. If I were a less rational man, I may even have come to the conclusion that the ocean didn't like me! A less rational man may have taken the attack personally. But of course, I realise that the ocean is the ocean just as rain is rain, and there is no negotiating with either.

You could argue, I suppose, that if I didn't like the water, I should have stayed on *terra firma*, but I will argue in turn! For what is a beach holiday without a dip in the sea?

I also found the beach just slightly too sandy. Now I do realise that may sound silly, but at a wonderful upmarket place like 'The Twin Palms Resort' I expected some kind of concession to be made for those of us who don't like sitting on sand. It does, after all, get into everything, and I'm certain I don't have to tell you that sand in a Speedo is no one's idea of fun!

The other half star was deducted because the staff, although extremely quick, kind, and courteous, insisted on speaking to each other in an 'African language'. I found this quite alarming, and disrespectful. They ought to be instructed that one should not do this in front of guests, as guests could possibly think they are gossiping about them and be unjustly (or justly!) offended.

I was unpleasantly reminded of my trip to Mallorca in '79 when *all* the staff spoke Spanish regardless of who they were addressing! Foreigners must be forgiven for trespasses like this, I suppose, as they weren't taught the manners and etiquette that are the imperative for the foundation of any good man. I must be forgiving of the shortcomings in their decorum in this regard: not everyone was lucky enough to have an Aunt Daphne to teach them these simple but essential courtesies that make the world a comfortable, dignified, and civilised place.

It goes without saying that *that* particular 'Spanish' establishment received considerably fewer stars than this glowing review. Although in those days there was no 'Trip Advisor' on the computer and I had to send a stamped letter in the post.

In addition to the hostile sea and babbling staff, I found the fishing at 'The Twin Palms Resort' wasn't up to much, which was a great pity as I had carted all of my new fishing gear along and didn't really make much use of it after the first day. Usually I'm known for some rather good catches, but these particular fish seemed to resist my superior right-wrist-flourish angling technique. It was disappointing, but I decided to pack it up and soldier on, and to not let it spoil my stay.

Lastly, while I found the hotel rooms were, on the whole, spacious and comfortable, I came to the conclusion that the walls were a little on the thin side. I could hear my neighbour talking on the phone while I made use of the ablution facilities. It goes without saying that it was quite disconcerting the first time it happened! As I sat down to read my newspaper I heard her say "Hello Darling!" and I almost jumped off the throne! Oh, I laughed when I saw her at breakfast that morning, although of course she wouldn't have known why.

Kind Regards,

Morgan Belafry, AKA Globetrotter69

Dear Mr Belafry

Since your stay here I have had various staff members approaching me to complain about your conduct as a guest at the Twin Palms. I feel it is important to address both your points and theirs.

You spoke of enjoying the traditional dancing and singing. I wonder if, next time, you could just stay seated and watch the entertainment from your table, as the other guests do, instead of leaping up every two minutes to grab the dancers and waltz them across the dining area, or slurring *your* version of *Nkosi Sikelel' iAfrika* at the top of your voice. (You may want to brush up on the lyrics, by the way. Moses told me that the words you were singing—and I use the term 'singing' loosely—were highly offensive to him and to the rest of the cultural group. He wouldn't go into detail, but he avoided eye contact with me when he relayed the story).

I also hasten to remind you that the point of the evening is to relax and appreciate the beautiful culture of the people who live in the area. It is not supposed to be a drunken karaoke free-for-all, hence our refusal to "give you the mic" as you demanded. Also, Moses would like his gumboots back.

On the topic of respecting the culture of the staff, we unapologetically reserve our staff's right to speak in their mother tongue. I wonder, Mr Belafry, why you think that people are gossiping behind your back? Is it perhaps because a small part of you knows that you deserve it? Do you really think it's unusual for people to talk about a hotel guest who has drunken arguments with himself in the middle of the night and then passes out in the early hours, only to snore like a bandsaw?

Perhaps, Mr Belafry, an old biblical phrase may apply here: you need to search for the log in your own eye before complaining about the splinter in ours. We had many problems with your stay here, and the fact that our staff speak vernacular is not one of them.

Regarding the 'complimentary' bar fridge in your room: it is labelled very clearly as an honesty bar, and there was a notebook on top of the appliance for you to record your consumption so that it could be added to your bill at the end of your stay. Nthabiseng, the cleaning lady responsible for your room, had to restock it daily, but didn't find any entries from you. Luckily, she made a note of the drinks you consumed and you'll be receiving the bill via email shortly. I have a feeling she was especially enthusiastic in regards to her record keeping, perhaps because she didn't appreciate the mess you left in your room every day, including, but not limited to: the odious bait box you insisted on keeping in the bedroom, the numerous occasions you flooded the bathroom despite our country-wide drought, and your insistence on calling her a 'girl' despite her being a woman in her thirties.

We do apologise for the fact that you could hear your neighbour talking on the phone. Nthabiseng told me she came in one morning to clean your room and found you holding a glass to the wall. I'll just leave that there.

Lastly, in response to your complaint about fishing, the Twin Palms beach is not a fishing area, and is signposted accordingly. There is a jetty a little further up the coast which is ideal for angling, and you'll find many local fisherman catching large fish there every day. If you had asked at reception or read your information booklet instead of using it as kindling in the *gas* fireplace in your room, you would have known this. I'm not surprised that you didn't catch anything, as the life guard told me you were casting into the tidal pool before she asked you to stop. I'm not sure what you were hoping to catch in there, but I was relieved to hear that no children were injured in the process.

I can assure you that the sea at our little beach does not have a vendetta against you, although to be honest, I wouldn't blame it, if it did. Also, for future reference, our beach is *not a swimming beach*. There are no shark nets protecting the area, and it's known for Great Whites, so it is really not a safe place to swim.

Kind regards

Vuleka Dandala, Manager, The Twin Palms Resort

∾

Trip Advisor Review: Twin Palms Resort. 2 out of 5 stars.

Well. I do have to wonder why such a wonderful holiday destination like 'The Twin Palms Resort' would have such an impertinent woman in charge of customer relations when she clearly has no idea of how one should speak to customers.

Ms Dandala, it is my opinion that your superior should remove you from your position immediately and replace you with someone who has experience in dealing with the minor niggles I believe should be addressed at your establishment. I am, after all, just trying to help! But I do understand that women (especially at certain times of the month) can take things personally when no direct offence is meant. Perhaps you could try to keep our communication civil and businesslike as befits your designation.

Further to my above recommendation, I also think that certain staff need replacing, namely, that housekeeping girl with the wild imagination, the reckless lifeguard at the beach, and Moses, primarily for not having a sense of humour.

For future reference, the last time I checked, this was a free country, and I will bloody well swim if I want to swim. How can you call yourself a beach resort when you don't allow guests to swim in the ocean? I find that absolutely ludicrous, and bad form all round.

And seeing as we are speaking in 'Biblical verses', here is one for you: Your mother was a hamster and your father smelt of elderberries.

I wish you good day!

Morgan Belafry, AKA @GlobeTrotter69

Dear Mr Belafry

I believe that verse is a Monty Python one, and not originally from the Bible. However, your sentiment is noted.

I'm glad you replied to my previous comment, allowing me to address some other issues which have since surfaced. Apart from the eye-watering bar fridge bill, we will also be sending you an account for the following: the bed slat you broke (I don't want to know how this happened); the toilet you blocked; the shaving mirror you cracked; and the swimming pool lilo you (perhaps mistakenly) took with you when you left. We will also be sending you a bill for the white towel you ruined. We can't tell if it's black hair dye or shoe polish but it used to be bright white and now it's irreversibly stained and we are holding you responsible for the cost of a new one.

I'm glad you've given us the opportunity to allow you to settle your debts. Thank you again for your original review which has made all of this possible, as we were able to track you and your contact details through your open profile page. The bill should reach you shortly. I do hope your credit card is no longer giving you problems.

Have a lovely day further.

Vuleka Dandala, Manager, The Twin Palms Resort

Trip Advisor Review: Twin Palms Resort. 0 out of 5 stars.

Listen here, Dandala. I have a biblical verse for you.

"I permit no woman to have authority over men; she is to keep silent." Timothy 2:11

Maybe old Tim had a point, ey? I mean, you may be a man-hating feminazi and believe that the world is a better place now with women in the working world but I can tell you that from my personal experience life was a lot more fun in the old days, when there was a race to space and women knew their place.

I find your communiqué blunt and spiteful, and I demand to speak to your manager about your flagrant and callous disregard for customers—and manners!—on the whole.

Mr Belafry

Dear Morgan

I will not rise to the 'feminazi' bait (which is, by the way, nonsensical, because you're basically equating someone who wants equal rights to someone who invaded Poland) and I'm pretty sure it was written during one of the midnight cursing sessions you seem to enjoy. I do hope you don't wreck your own home in the same way you do hotel rooms. I can't help but wonder if your Aunt Daphne ever taught you any manners whatsoever, or if you just ignored her in the same way you seem to disregard common decency.

So even although your comment was silly and not worth this response, I am typing it anyway just to let you know that I am passing this customer service nightmare over to my boss, the owner of the hotel group, because I honestly have more important things to do than to deal with the deluded ravings of a drunken, idiotic lunatic.

Vuleka

PS.

I'm not sure if I mentioned this before, but when I asked the lifeguard on the beach why she didn't report you for exposing yourself to the other beachgoers, she just shrugged and said "There was nothing to see."

But don't be upset, Belafry, look at it this way: you're lucky to have a one-inch wonder, or you might have had a criminal case on your hands.

Sayonara, my little gherkin. I'll always remember you when I look at our fresh salad buffet bar.

~

Trip Advisor Review: Twin Palms Resort. 0 out of 5 stars.

I will not dignify that childish jibe with a response, except to say I am glad that I'll finally be in correspondence with someone who knows how to treat customers!

Goodbye, you ill-mannered plebeian, and, as Aunt Doris would have said: Good Riddance!

~

Dear Globetrotter 69

The manager at The Twin Palms Resort, Vuleka Dandala, has escalated this review thread to me, the owner of the hotel group, to put to bed. I do hope we can come to an understanding and close these comments off for good. As you can see it has become quite a popular thread and we are getting tweets and emails from all over the world about your review. In fact, I see you have quite a following, with your string of strident reviews. It is becoming an untenable situation as we are being bombarded by well-meaning members of the public with their supportive comments and it's taking up all our digital (and psychological) bandwidth.

As you seem to be fond of biblical metaphors, allow me to extend one to you in the form of an olive branch.

As the owner of the Golden Beach Hotel Group I'd like to offer you a unique deal. If you agree to never visit any of our resorts ever again, we will forgive your debt and call our lawyers off. This includes all of our current establishments and any future ventures, too, so including but not limited to:

Sunset Beach Hotel

Gate Bridge B&B

Oceania Overnight

Twin Palms Resort

Lakeside Lodges, and

Coconut Bungalows

I trust that you will take us up on our generous offer, and we will not cross paths again.

Sincerely,

The Golden Beach Hotel Group (PTY) LTD.

Dear 'Golden Beach Hotel Group'

Thank you for your polite response and generous offer. I accept it with gratitude. As my Aunt Daphne used to say, "You shouldn't look a gift horse in the mouth." I didn't know then what a gift horse was (nor do I now), but I certainly won't be looking at this one in the mouth (or elsewhere!).

Best

Morgan Belafry AKA @GlobeTrotter69

OMG.

That's you, Travelling Slacks! That's you, isn't it?-You and your Aunt bloody Daphne!

It's Suzy Dos Santos here, owner of the hotel group.

We've been trying to track you down for ages, trying to get a warrant for your arrest for theft and property damage at our other hotels—specifically Coconut Bungalows—but we've never been able to locate your residential address.

But now we have it! Now we've got you, you wily bastard. And all because you had the temerity to leave a substandard review.

I can't wait to see you in court.

OMG. OMG.

I've been going through the older reviews linked to your profile and I see that, apart from @TravellingSlacks, you catfish as Nelson Smith, Boris Y @Yell2Soon, @CrabCatcher55 and David de la Haye @Makin'Hey. How many online identities do you have?

We followed the trail from your profile but the address you listed took us to an abandoned building. The investigator said it was disgusting: newspaper piled to the ceiling and rotten food in the fridge; rats; and a swarm of cockroaches. I knew it must have been your old place when they told me about the old, broken violin.

You're a serial one-star reviewer and you've trashed every single one of our hotels. What is your obsession with our group?

Let me warn you right now that we will not tolerate any further communication from you or any of your fake online personas. You'd better leave me alone, Jeff Sacks, or Morgan Belafry, or whatever your bloody name is. I never want to hear from you again. You stay away from me, my staff, and my business.

PS.

I've alerted the police to your insane behaviour and we're in the process of filing a restraining order. If I were you I'd disappear and never, ever contact me again, or you'll be very sorry. I have a team of expensive lawyers and I am not afraid to use them.

Oh, Suzy, so lovely to hear from you again. I wondered when you'd recognise my style of writing. I have been told that I have a distinct 'voice' and a special flair for composition.

Then I found myself wondering if you'd somehow recognise me in the flesh, even though we've never officially met before. But I know your face so well by now and would recognise you anywhere, even though you often change the colour of your hair. I do like the current shade, by the way. That burnished brown is fetching on you. It looked especially good with that navy blouse you were wearing this morning. I like your perfume, too. Is it new? I thought it smelled delicious. It gets five stars from me.

Dear Mister Belafry / Sacks

This CEASE AND DESIST ORDER is to inform you that your persistent actions including but not limited to harassing Mrs Suzy Dos Santos have become unbearable. You are ORDERED TO STOP such activities immediately as they are being done in violation of the law.

Mrs Dos Santos has the right to remain free from these activities as they constitute harassment and stalking, and we will pursue any legal remedies available to us against you if these activities continue. These remedies include contacting law enforcement to obtain criminal sanctions against you, and suing you civilly for the damages that Mrs Dos Santos and The Golden Beach Hotel Group (PTY) LTD have incurred as a result of your actions.

You risk incurring severe legal consequences if you fail to comply with this demand.

This letter acts as your final warning to discontinue this unwanted conduct before we pursue legal actions against you.

Sincerely,

Mr David Jankowitz (LLB)

Jankowitz and Associates

On behalf of The Golden Beach Hotel Group (PTY) LTD

~

The host server @GlobeTrotter69 is not recognised. This email address has been deleted. This message will not be re-sent. This is a permanent error message.

~

5

COURT, MARRY, KILL

Even in the dread dark of the ocean floor, it didn't take long for the scavengers to find the body. A cast of crabs arrived first, then a risk of lobsters. The shrimp showed up, too. First they nibbled at the softer parts, the eyeballs and the split lip, but soon they unzipped the skin and opened up the body for the smaller creatures to feast. In less than three weeks the body was stripped to the bone, and now an ivory skeleton's empty orbs stare up at the ocean's rippling surface, forever fading away into the cold, dark floor.

CURTIS

She wasn't like the other girls. I watched her as she smiled at customers, brought plates of food, wiped down tables with the damp cloth that smelt of bleach she kept in a little plastic bag in the pocket of her apron, which was a navy blue and made her eyes look like stars on velvet.

I used to only go out for breakfast once a month. That's my budget. At Croissant&Co I'm allowed to order one small juice and a breakfast special (it comes with a free coffee). But when Monica started waitressing there I began making excuses to visit the restaurant more often.

I was in the neighbourhood, I would tell her, which, strictly speaking, was true: I lived three blocks away from where she worked. When she spoke quietly to me, the faintest blush on her cheeks, I'd feel so energised. I started to get the idea that I could be anything, do anything, with her and God by my side. The other girls wore vulgar short skirts and painted their lips with brash colours, but Monica had true beauty. She didn't need to show off, or pretend. The thing that struck me when I first met her was the streak of vulnerability that lies under her skin like a silver vein. She was just so beautiful and open and tender. I instantly wanted to take her under my wing. Hold her, protect her, love her like she's never been loved before.

"Can I get you another coffee?" she said, a ribbon of hair falling over her eye. She smiled apologetically and quickly clipped it back in place.

A second coffee wasn't in my budget, but how could I have refused? I threw caution to the wind.

"Yes, please."

It's not like I don't have the money. I have plenty of money, I just like to be careful with it. When Monica brought my coffee —black, with hot milk, just the way I like it—my breath caught in my throat and I had to fight the urge to cough. It was a moment I'd been thinking about for weeks. Months. My bathroom mirror was already sick of hearing the speech.

"I was wondering," I said, trying to keep my voice even. I cleared my throat. "Monica?"

Monica gave me one of her most generous smiles, and that gave me courage to continue.

"I was wondering if you'd like to grab a drink, sometime."

Her smile faltered and there was confusion in her eyes. My heart shrivelled right then; my face tingled with shame. Oh, what had I been thinking! Of course this magnificent woman was too good for me.

I started rambling. "I completely understand if you'd rather not—"

"I'd love to!" she said, and relief coursed through my veins.

We exchanged numbers and I floated out of the restaurant. Magnificent Monica. I was on cloud nine for the rest of the day.

MONICA

Our first date was beyond incredible. Curtis took me for a drink at that swanky bar in Clifton that overlooks the sea. I ordered a candyfloss G&T and it was amazing, then we went to sit on the beach and I felt intoxicated by the drink and the fizzing ocean and the fact that I was sitting next to Curtis Brennan. Curtis Brennan!

When I started working at Croissant and he came in for his breakfast, the other girls would giggle. They told me who he was, said they'd sell their souls for a date with him. He was perfect: sweet, rich and good looking, we dreamed of him being our ticket out of our ordinary drab lives in the restaurant, scraping leftover food off plates and cleaning up other people's broken glass. We fantasised about sunning ourselves on his shiny white yacht in the middle of the bright blue sea.

And then I was sitting right next to him, and we were talking, *really* talking, and it was all so surreal and real at the same time that my head was spinning. The sand was warm, the sun began to melt into the sea, and the dusk painted his face orange and pink. His hair looked dark, his eyes full of light, and in that moment it was like my life changed forever. We both knew it was the beginning of something—something important—and I knew I'd never forget that day.

CURTIS

Monica is perfect. Just perfect. Things are going exactly according to plan. On Friday nights I pick her up after her lunch shift and we go out. I take her anywhere she wants to go and let her order whatever she's in the mood for. It's tearing a hole in my budget but I just tell myself that our courtship won't always be that expensive. It's an investment in our future.

We talk for hours, sometimes late into the night. Usually I make sure I get at least seven and a half hours of sleep, but when I'm with Monica I get to bed really late and then still toss and turn, thinking of her. Sometimes I don't even read my bible anymore. I lie there picturing her flawless face, her exquisite body. Not that I've ever seen her body; not naked, anyway. I make sure that I'm the perfect gentleman. She deserves no less.

I wake up exhausted, but energised. I know that sounds nonsensical, but it's true. It's like my brain is tired, but my heart is on fire. There is new hope and purpose in every day.

MONICA

Curtis and I are officially a couple. When he picks me up from work the other girls giggle and wave, and Mick, our manager, tells us to *Have fun, kids!* Even though I think he might be younger than Curtis. Curtis doesn't like Mick, says he knows restaurant managers and they're usually less than respectful to their staff. I don't know about that. Mick's always been very kind to me. Curtis says he doesn't like the way Mick looks at me. I honestly can't tell. He looks at me just like all the other men do. Just like Curtis does.

Curtis wants me to stop waitressing at Croissant, says that I deserve better than that, but I need the money. Tuition fees for my final year at UCT will be due in January and I don't even have half of the money I need for that. I need to keep working.

CURTIS

Am I wrong about Monica? I thought she was different. I thought she was pure. And then I found her in a clinch with that godawful man at the restaurant and my head exploded. I was so angry that I couldn't think straight. Angry that it happened, angry about what it could mean, and furious that they made me lose control like that.

MONICA

Oh. My. God.

Sitting in casualty with Curtis because he has a fractured hand. He came to pick me up early from Croissant&Co and I was in the back room with Mick. I was asking him if I could double up on some of my shifts and he um-ed and ah-ed and looked at the schedule. Said there wasn't really much more available, and then I told him what the money was for and his eyes softened and said *Sure, we can squeeze a few more shifts in.* I was so happy I hugged him, and it felt really nice, and that's when Curtis came flying in and he punched Mick so hard that he broke his hand! I was completely in shock, I honestly couldn't believe what had just happened. Then Curtis grabbed me and shoved me out of the back room, out of the restaurant, while Mick was holding a restaurant napkin to his bleeding face and shouting about calling the police. I had to drive Curtis to the hospital, and it made him even more angry that he couldn't do it himself. He hasn't spoken to me since.

I keep telling him what really happened between Mick and I (nothing!) but I can see he doesn't believe me. I don't blame him for thinking that. I mean, it must have looked pretty suspect when he came in and saw us hugging like that. All the girls at the restaurant pretend to flirt with Mick. We bat our eyelashes at him and blow kisses. Not often, but it does happen. It's just a joke, a silly game, to make the time pass. To make sure we don't die of boredom in between filling coffees and bringing bills. The hug was totally innocent, but now I feel ashamed. I shouldn't have hugged him, and I definitely shouldn't have enjoyed it.

CURTIS

My hand is healing nicely. Luckily my medical aid paid the

hospital bills, which made it easier for me to forgive Monica. It all turned out rather well, because now Monica no longer works at Croissant. Now she doesn't have to serve people and clean up their mess, or hang around that terrible gaggle of half-wits she used to call her friends. Mick pretended to be a Good Guy about the whole thing; said he wouldn't press charges if I never went back there. He said Monica was welcome to work there again if she gave me the boot, but of course that wasn't an option. My love chose me. Can you believe that? She chose me.

MONICA

I had decided, sitting there in casualty, that I'd break up with Curtis. The whole thing just made me feel so sick to my stomach. I was so sad and so nervous, I felt like my emotions were all clawing up my throat and it made it very difficult to speak. I didn't want to end things. I mean, I'm falling in love with him! But how can I love a man who loses his temper like that? That was crazy. And not just any crazy. Batshit crazy! And then he didn't speak to me for ages afterwards and I just felt my heart harden against him. He's not the man I thought he was. Or, rather, he's not the man he was pretending to be.

Also, breaking up with Curtis is the only way I'll get my job back, and god knows I need the money. As it is I'm a week late on my rent and the agent called, saying I'm in breach of contract. They'll chuck out my stuff and change the locks at the end of the month if I don't come up with the cash ASAP.

But then yesterday Curtis arrived at my flat while I was ironing my Croissant apron—I'd had to hand-wash it to get rid of the blood—and I was thinking maybe I shouldn't let him in, but there he stood with this gigantic bunch of flowers and a look of outright contrition on his face and my resolve melted. I mean, no one is perfect, right? And it's not like I was completely innocent.

He's never hit someone before, he doesn't know what came over him, he said. He just saw Mick and I hugging and thought the worst, thought that Mick was taking advantage of me, and he just 'saw red' and next thing his fist was flying towards Mick's face. It's because he's so much in love with me, he said.

Which made me happy but sad, because I was planning on telling him that I loved him before what happened in the back room and I was hoping he would say it back, maybe while we were looking at the moon or sitting on the beach again. I don't know. Doing something romantic.

He could see I was still wary, so he was extra nice to me, took the iron away and held my hand, asked how everything was. And then I don't know why, I guess it was his kindness or sympathy or something but I just started crying. I had been so upset about the incident and so stressed about not having a job anymore but I had been holding it all in, trying to be strong. But Curtis's eyes, his beautiful light-filled eyes that I know so well, looked deep into mine and I just crumbled.

He kissed the tears off my cheeks and held me so tightly, telling me everything was going to be okay. That he would take care of everything.

And he meant *everything*. Curtis offered to pay the rent I was behind on, and to then pay for a moving company. I was, like, *a moving company?* And then it dawned on me: *Curtis was asking me to move in with him!*

It makes sense, he said. I would no longer have to pay rent or wait on people. I could live at his place and concentrate on my studies. He'd even pay for my varsity tuition for next year. I couldn't believe it. I was so grateful I started crying again, and he picked me up and carried me to bed. I was so relieved, but I also had a small nagging thought that wouldn't go away. The flowers, the apology, the promise that 'it will never happen again'—I've heard that all before, right? In woman's magazines and American soap operas. I know how those stories end. But Curtis isn't like that. I've never felt safer than that moment, as he carried me in his strong arms. I knew he would do anything to protect me.

Curtis lay down with me on my bed, both of us fully clothed, and cuddled me until I stopped crying. When I woke up, he was gone.

CURTIS

I was hoping it wouldn't come to this, but I need to force her hand.

I was watching Monica talk to some students on the campus and I couldn't stand the way she was acting. She was laughing and smiling—her brightest smile—and swinging her hips like the town tramp. She was going to wear a skirt, but I told her she looks better in jeans. I'm glad she took my advice. She was so cheerful that morning before the orientation class, irritatingly so, and she had hugged me hard and thanked me again for paying for her university fees. I like that, having that power over her, but then when I saw her with the other men I knew it wasn't going to work. No, that wasn't going to work at all.

MONICA

I'm going to get married!! I know I'm a little young—Dad's going to flip his lid— but maybe when he meets Curtis he'll see how lucky I am? We're going to court next month and his priest will attend. Curtis doesn't want a big wedding. He doesn't like parties, and he says that weddings are just a grandiose way to waste money. I'm a little sad about that, to be honest, I mean, I'd love to have a big wedding! But Curtis is right when he says that we don't need anything but each other. It's what true love is about. I'm going to buy a beautiful white dress, though, I don't care what he says. Marriage is, after all, about negotiation, right? Give and take. He gets his way with the wedding, and I get the dress.

My friends are all super jealous, say I've hit the jackpot, but Curtis says the opposite is true. That he's the one who scooped the first prize. I wonder if his friends feel the same. Funny thing is, he doesn't seem to have many friends. Just business contacts and customers. I've never really thought about that before. I would say that my friends would become his friends, but I think they're a little immature for him. Whenever I drag him along to some art gallery or something he doesn't talk much and his eyes grow cold. Like, why would a successful businessman want to hang around a bunch of liberal students who wear too much eyeliner and drink box wine.

In the meantime I'm practising. I try to keep the house clean and do the washing. I'm quite enjoying it, actually! But I expect the novelty will wear off soon. Curtis likes me to do the grocery shopping and cook dinner now that I'm not working anymore and he's basically paying for everything. The cooking part isn't working out, because even though I warned him that I'm not good in the kitchen, he gets really annoyed when I burn the food. Says the takeaways we eat are making me fat. I guess it's just something we'll have to iron out after the wedding.

I'm super nervy / excited about our wedding night. Can you believe we've never had sex? In this day and age! But Curtis insists. He wants to be the prefect gentleman. Every now and then I try to tempt him, try to unbutton his shirt while we're watching Netflix or surprise him by not wearing panties under my dress at dinner at one of those fancy restaurants he used to take me to, but he just keeps quiet and shakes his head. He's so old fashioned like that, but it's cool in a way, you know?

CURTIS

Today is the happiest day of my life. I am so blessed. I married Monica! She was so glowing and so beautiful in her white dress. I can't believe she belongs to me. When I slipped the wedding ring on her finger I felt like the luckiest man in the world. Her family is impressed that we're going sailing for our honeymoon. It'll be Monica's first trip on my yacht. I can't wait to show her the ropes.

MONICA

When we were in court and it was time to exchange rings, my ring stuck a little over my knuckle and Curtis just forced it on. When I gasped that it was sore, he glared at me as if to say *Shut up! You'll embarrass me!* And my cheeks burned when I remembered all the times he had asked me to watch my weight before the wedding. But I've not put on too much weight—three kilos at the most—honestly I just think he made the ring too small (maybe so that I wouldn't be able to take it off?). So I just gulped the pain down and kept quiet and tried to forget about it—I didn't want to spoil the special day by starting a fight—but then things got worse.

I was so excited about our wedding night AND taking out the yacht for the first time. It was like my dream of sailing into the sunset with Curtis was coming true.

Curtis had put so much thought and effort into the trip. He packed a huge picnic basket full of food, and he put a bottle of MCC Brut on ice. He laid out a big white tablecloth on the floor with pillows and we sat down together. Yellow plums and strawberries and salmon, all kinds of beautiful cheeses and salted crackers. My favourite Swiss chocolate. After my second glass of bubbly I began to relax and really enjoy it (before I was too nervous!).

I thought maybe we'd go to bed, because Curtis is proper like that, but then he took my glass out of my hand and started kissing me, and the next thing we were making love on the make-shift picnic blanket, which sounds super romantic but the floor was actually hard and uncomfortable. I pretended to enjoy it, though, because a wedding night is not something you forget, and it was over quickly, anyway.

Afterwards I thought he'd lie with me while we held hands and talked about the future, but instead he checked the tablecloth underneath me and asked where the blood was.

The blood? I asked. I was confused. Then it hit me. Curtis thought I was a virgin. I explained that I wasn't, and he called me a liar and slapped me so hard that I blacked out. When I came to he was shouting at me, saying that I was a slut and a liar. I crept up into the corner and tried to make myself as small as possible, wiping the blood from my nose, and waiting for him to calm down. I've never seen someone so angry or out of control in my life.

I just kept thinking *what have I done, what have I done?* until he eventually went to bed and I passed out on the hard floor.

CURTIS

Monica betrayed me, but I think we can still make it work. We're married now, after all, and I'm willing to give her another chance. Till death do us part, right?

MONICA

Today I tried to attend my first class of the year but the security guard wouldn't let me in. He took away my student card. I was sure it was a mistake and I phoned the faculty. It appears that Curtis has withdrawn my tuition funding. In fact, he hadn't made any payment whatsoever, so my enrolment fell through, and now there are no more places left.

CURTIS

Monica's a little upset about my decision about her studies. I'm not sure why. I thought it would be clear to her, when I asked her to marry me, that she would no longer need to attend university. I have enough money for both of us. While I toil away, she never has to do anything! She doesn't know how lucky she is. Anyway, I'm sure she'll come round. She always does.

MONICA

When people hear about abusive relationships they say "Why didn't she leave?"

I'll tell you why.

The last time I tried to leave Curtis he found me and broke my left collarbone and I couldn't drive for weeks. That was my sixth visit to casualty in as many months, and the nursing staff have started to ask me questions. I just tell them I'm clumsy. If I told them the truth they'd think I was stupid for staying, but they don't know what Curtis is capable of.

They don't know that if I try to leave him again, he'll kill me. So the nurses just squeeze my hand in sympathy and surreptitiously pass me extra painkillers—the really strong, post-operative ones—and tell me they guess they'll be seeing me again soon. I have a little pile of the pills now, and I close my eyes and think of them when Curtis is climbing into me.

I keep the hospital bands, the pills, and a secret wallet of pilfered cash which I add to as often as I can. I may not be able to leave, but I can dream about it. The hope keeps me alive.

Despite this, I feel myself slipping into depression. Curtis doesn't like it when I leave the house, so I can't exercise or see my friends. They probably just think I'm so happy that I don't have time for them anymore. And when I do feel brave—brave enough to quickly nip outside—I feel ashamed of the bruises that splatter my skin and I decide to rather stay in. It's safer, I tell myself. It's safer, even though the opposite is true.

I've started boxing lessons. I watch YouTube tutorials while Curtis is at work and listen to 80s music while I practice and practice, sometimes for hours at a time, punching thin air, or a pillow wrapped up in a blanket. I know how to make a proper fist, now, and how to bob and weave. It makes me feel stronger, even though, when faced with Curtis's temper, my mind goes blank and I'd never actually dare to fight back. I think fighting back would be a one-way ticket.

I keep practising, anyway.

CURTIS

Monica is really being so troublesome. Sometimes I wonder if this whole thing has been a mistake. Why can't she just be a good wife? Is it really so difficult? I do so much for her and she just lies around the house. I asked her the other day what happened to her. She's supposed to be a housewife but she doesn't even know how to clean up. Never mind the housework, she doesn't even shower anymore! Her hair is a greasy mess. She doesn't even look at me when I talk to her. She's disgusting, a total disgrace. I still make love to her, but it's just not the same.

MONICA

Living with Curtis is like living with a drunk, raging bear. All day, I try to disappear. I try to fade into walls. I flinch when he comes near me, flinch when he talks. But nowadays even flinching can get me hurt. I try to keep myself as unattractive as possible, but he rapes me anyway. Now he just tells me how dirty and ugly I am while he's doing it.

CURTIS

The funniest thing happened. When I got home from work today, Monica had showered and put make-up on, and she was even wearing a clean dress. She's thankfully lost a bit of weight in the last few months, so she was looking really good. The house was clean, the laundry ironed, and, wait for it, there was even a home cooked meal on the table! And candles! I couldn't believe it. What has caused this seismic shift? Has she finally come to her senses? I was so impressed I couldn't help but hug her. She flinched, and I felt the first sparks of anger, but then I took a deep breath of her freshly shampooed hair and forgave her. Love is generous. Love is kind. God has brought my beautiful wife back to me.

While we were eating, she put down her knife and fork and looked me in the eyes. They're still beautiful eyes, despite the scars she insists on wearing.

She said she wanted us to start again.

She explained that she knows more about me and our relationship now, and will know how to behave in the right way. Well, what can I say, I am beyond thrilled. I said yes, yes, of course, and then she asked if we can have a second honeymoon, a night on the yacht, to celebrate. She said she's even been brushing up on her sailing lessons. I was floored. I think it's a terrific idea. It will be symbolic of our second chance. I was in a generous, jovial mood, so I opened a second bottle of wine.

I'm already scheming about what to put in the picnic basket this time around.

MONICA

We sailed out at dusk. I was wearing a new dress, one I knew Curtis would like. Not too revealing, but showing off my figure really nicely, in a beautiful deep blue, hinting at the night that was to come. I haven't seen Curtis that happy for a long time. He kept saying how brilliant my idea was, how clever I was, how pretty, how magnificent. I nodded and gave him my brightest smile, *Yes,* I said, *a new beginning.* And that's what we toasted to on the bow deck as the ocean rippled around us, salt scenting the air.

As Curtis drained his second glass, he pulled his lips a little to the side, and frowned into the champagne flute. His brain was still trying to make sense of the bitter aftertaste of the champagne when I smashed my fist into his nose as hard as I could. He dropped the glass and it shattered on the deck, and his hands went flying up to his face. His lip was split, his nose gushed with blood. As his shock turned into rage, he lost his balance. The drugs were making him sleepy; dizzy. He lunged for me but I easily sidestepped him, and then using his momentum, I pushed him over the side of the boat, and heard his body hit the water with a splash. I watched him flail around in the black water, shouting for help, and when the shouting faded and his head finally tipped under the surface, I waited to make sure he wouldn't climb up and back inside. Then I got the brush and pan and I cleaned up the broken flute, and threw it overboard, the glass shards like diamonds on velvet. I wiped up the blood with a solution of bleach and threw that into the sea, too, and imagined it sinking all the way down to join my husband on the dark ocean floor.

It seems I can clean up well, after all.

6

CAN WE LIGHT A FIRE?

"CAN WE LIGHT A FIRE?" I ask my dad. "Can we light a fire?"

Because:

1. I love lighting fires, and

2. You have to ask twice or three times. Once doesn't work, and four times is unlucky. I try to be lucky. Three is the luckiest number.

There are lots of ways you can be lucky, but more ways you can be unlucky.

If you need more luck in your day you can wear red socks or red underpants. If you wear red socks *and* red undies, watch out world! The day is yours. Also, make sure your hair is clean (but not too clean) and that you've done your face exercises in the bathroom mirror. Smile, frown, gasp, pull a funny face, in that order, three times. Never four times. If you make a mistake and do it four times, then you have to do it six times altogether, because that's two times three, and those are both lucky numbers.

"Can we light a fire, Dad?"

Dad lowers his newspaper and I can only see his eyes. He's thinking.

He's thinking that he's busy reading, but he wouldn't mind lighting a fire with me. He likes fires, too. Sometimes we make a big fire in the garden, in the fire pit, and I watch the orange flames on his glasses.

He's thinking that it would be a good thing to do, except that maybe it would encourage my love of fire, which he wouldn't want to do.

She's a pyromaniac, he'd joke with his friends, and they'd all laugh and nod, but then they'd look uncomfortable, as if I would burn the house down while they're all sitting there, drinking their gin and tonics. Which is really silly, because why would I burn my own house down? That would be very unlucky.

Dad looks at his silver watch and then back at me.

Maybe he's wondering when Mom will be home from visiting Aunt Jax. Mom doesn't like it when I light fires. She says I don't understand how dangerous it is (I do). She says one day I'll hurt someone with my fire-setting.

I stand as still as a statue and look at Dad. I can't ask again. I have to wait for him to decide.

"All right," he says, and gets up. He removes the advert section of the newspaper and shakes the remaining pages, then folds them neatly and presses them down. I like it when he does that.

He has other neat habits that I like:

1. He butters his toast all the way to the edge.

2. He polishes the kitchen counter till it shines, and

3. He sleeps on the left side of the bed.

I don't like it when he cuts himself shaving and then sticks a piece of tissue on to the cut. Blood is unlucky, and so are curse words, so shaving accidents are very unlucky.

Dad stretches up for the fire-lighting box on the top shelf in the kitchen larder and brings it down. They always put it out of my reach but one day I'll be tall enough to get it on my own. We go out into the garden and the sun is hot on my hair and my back, but I don't mind, because we're going to light a fire.

I go around the garden collecting kindling. I don't have to—we have fire-lighters—but I like to use dry twigs and newspaper. I like it starting off small and then feeding it and watching it grow bigger.

When I was four I almost burnt down the timber wendy house.

Gran gave me a toy oven for Christmas and it was perfect for the playhouse. I had small pots and pans and spoons, and a pair of tongs with an alligator face. I liked the new toy but I wanted it to work like a real oven. I wanted to look through the clear perspex door and see the orange light; wanted to feel the warmth on my face. I watched my parents for days until there was a gap where I could quickly snatch some matches before they noticed. My hands were shaking and I almost dropped the box on the floor, but I managed to push it into my pocket without them noticing it was gone. I had an old YOU magazine inside the oven which I had already crumpled up a bit, so it was ready to be lit as soon as I had something to light it with. Still trembling, it took four matches to light, and by then I already knew it would be bad. I knew I should have stopped, but it's like my body just kept moving to light the thin pages even though my brain was saying that four matches are never a good sign. Four matches are a very bad sign.

The magazine whooshed beautifully into flames, and I felt so good watching it, knowing that I was the person who had created such a pretty thing. It was as if the oven was real, and alive, and it was one of the most satisfying things I've ever felt.

But then things got bad, as I guessed they would. The oven caught alight, and the flames leapt to the red-and-white checked curtain over the window. I had a bucket of water ready, but I hadn't counted on the fire spreading so fast. The water doused most of the oven but the flames jumped from the curtains to the dry timber roof. I ran to get more water, but the tap was so slow and I could hear the fire crackling behind me. Smoke was billowing out of the doorway. I rushed back with the water, sloshing most of it on my short legs on the way over, and splashed it over the burning curtains. It took three more buckets before the fire was completely out. Exhausted, coughing, and blackened with soot, I lay on the wet floor and closed my eyes, remembering the beauty of the flames licking the oven door, then the fabric, then the ceiling. The feeling of panic, of wildness, then relief. I lay there out of breath and exhausted and knowing that I'd do it again.

"You ready?" says Dad, and I nod.

He had decided we'd use the kettle braai: The smart, shiny domed barbecue grill he had recently bought. I think it's a good move because Mom will be less cross if there's a reason for the fire; if she doesn't need to cook dinner. I start by laying out some of Dad's newspaper and the small sticks, then put the coals on top. I like doing it neatly, even though the fire will mangle it. Fire doesn't care about neatness, or how you butter your toast.

When I was six I stole a lighter from a teacher at school. Mrs Delport had carelessly left it on the bannister where she would smoke at break time, and as I was walking past, it was like a little hot siren blaring at me. I had no choice but to take it; it was waiting especially for me. Plus, it was red, which is like wearing a label that says *Lucky*, and I needed luck that day, because my best friend, Emma, wasn't playing with me, and I was wearing grey underpants.

Having the lighter changed everything, because I didn't have to wait for my parents to accidentally leave some matches lying around, which they hardly ever did, after the playhouse incident. My lighter was like a magic tool. I could light anything, any time. It gave me such a powerful feeling.

I started in the guest bathroom at home. I thought it would be the safest place, covered in beige tiles that can't catch fire. I would light scraps of paper in the basin and watch them burn and transform into ribbons of black ash. I'd burn different things to see how their flames compared: Orange, blue, red. My favourite was green, because it was unusual. Some things hissed with sparks, and some smoked a lot.

Next I'd spray the air freshener (Scent of Strawberries) and light that, which would result in a very satisfying *whoosh* and a fire-ball big enough to shock and please me every time. When I wanted to get closer to the fire then I'd go into my mom's vanity cupboard and find her hairspray. I'd spray it all over my arms and then set them alight. I used to love that; watching the blue flames dancing on my arms, popping and hissing. I'd do this in the bath so that as soon as I felt the fire start to eat through the lacquer and burn my skin I'd just lower my arms into the bath water. I'd never intentionally burn myself or anyone else, although of course accidents do happen.

Dad lets me use the long lighter, which has a small cartridge of paraffin and a trigger like a gun. He watches as I click it and hold the small orange flame to the balled-up newspaper. The fire starts slowly, timidly, just hungry enough for one piece of paper, then it reaches for the dry twig above it. When I see fire, especially one I've lit myself, it's like there is light in my dark-ness, the darkness that has always been with me, deep inside my body and my heart. The flames are so beautiful. I look up at Dad, wondering if he's thinking the same thing, but he's looking at me with a worried expression. He clicks the knuckles on his right hand, which he does when he's anxious, then takes the lighter away from me with a tight smile.

"I'm going inside to marinate the meat," he says. "Don't touch the fire."

"I won't."

I step closer and lean into the warmth. Dad goes inside and taps on the glass, which makes me jump. "I'm going to watch you through the kitchen window."

I nod. I resist the strong temptation to play with the fire. I just stand and watch it burn.

When Mom comes home she pulls me towards her and smells smoke on my dress. She checks that the fire box is tucked safely away and strokes my hair. She's happy to not have to cook.

Fifteen Years Later

I hold the drip torch in my gloved hand and watch as the fire pours out of it and onto the dry grass and veld. Liquid fire, like magic, pools and leaps and dances behind me as I walk. The fuel is part gasoline, part diesel, 30% to 70%, which are good numbers, and the drip torch is red, which is lucky. It's funny because it looks a bit like a fire extinguisher, but it does the opposite job. The burning wick lights the fuel as it pours out and splashes flames on the ground. It makes me feel insanely happy, and powerful, and reminds me of the looted lighter I had when I was a kid.

There is a crash behind me, and I look around to see what has happened. A tall tree has succumbed to the fire and fallen down. Its fiery branches act as firelighters to the surrounding grass, which crackle immediately with flames. I see the fire I have set reach higher and higher, until it climbs the boughs of the other, bigger trees, and seeks to bring them down, too.

The smoke stings my nose and eyes, and my spirit soars. I want to dance to the sizzling and snapping of the glowing wood. Birds cry and launch themselves into the sky, into safety. I hope the other animals have found refuge, too. I try not to think of the rabbits, the squirrels, the sleeping owls. Butterflies with flames for wings.

I've lit a path of two kilometres now, and my efforts blaze behind me as if I have left a trail of golden footsteps. I'm exhausted from the effort and the excitement, and it reminds me of the day I sprawled out on the soaking, smoking floor of the playhouse.

I hear the firetruck as it comes my way, rolling over bushes and flattening dead wood. I turn off the torch and put it down next to me. When they get close enough to see me I put up my hands.

They roll forward and a couple of men jump off the back and shout. They come right up to me and smack my heavy gloved palms with theirs. They whoop with pleasure at the fire rushing from behind us.

The fire chief is quiet, but he nods at me. We have been successful. This is the last of three backfires that will cut off the fuel for the raging main fire that has been engulfing the side of the mountain for two days. Today, the third firebreak will cut it off. It'll die down into black stones and fragrant ashes. No more houses will be lost to it, no more lives. I knew it would work. Three is the luckiest number.

~

7

HE DID IT

THE VICTIM.

The victim drove a '66 Cadillac De Ville convertible with fender skirts and cracked upholstery. That's what you get for driving a cabriolet in Africa. Cracked leather seats that will pinch your ass and a dash so brittle it looks like it'll shatter if you punch it. I look down at my knuckles: scarred and blotchy, like hills blighted with drought. Maybe I should stop punching dashboards.

What the hell was he doing with a Cadillac, anyway? Cadillacs are for wide open roads and happy neighbours, drive-ins and Coke Floats and roller derbies. Cheerleaders snapping pink elastic bubble gum, and middle-aged businessmen in bright ties, sweating; smoking cigars. The man should have known this car has no place in a city like Jo'burg, with its grey skyscrapers and piss-grubby bridges and blistering sun and pedestrians who will knife you for your phone.

The car sticks out like a sore thumb. Like a bright blue sore thumb. What is that colour, anyway? Duck egg? Teal?

"Aqua," says Dom. "It's aqua."

Dom's lying on the car's bonnet like a pin-up girl, except he's hairy, and wearing an Italian suit.

"Ah," I say. "Yes. Aqua."

Or, it used to be aqua, anyway. The fingerprint team attacked the vehicle so enthusiastically it looks like Pablo Escobar sneezed.

"Is all the snow really necessary?" I ask them. They just frown at me. They're always getting into trouble. People are always phoning the station saying THEY DIDN'T EVEN DUST FOR FINGERPRINTS so now they're generous with the powder and don't clean up afterwards. Who can blame them? I don't. Who cares if they leave the crime scene looking like a festive season showdown at a shopping mall? Inspecting the photographs entered into evidence you'd think Father Christmas had been strewing dead bodies all over the city. Serial Killer Santa.

Domino starts whistling a Christmas carol. I think it's a carol, anyway. It makes me think of that acrid smell of a spent cracker: potassium nitrate, charcoal, sulphur. There's nothing quite like the smell of gunpowder to celebrate the festive season.

"The word *cabriolet* originally comes from the French language," says Dom.

He's in a philosophical mood, I can tell.

"Mid 18th century. *Cabriole* is a goat's leap."

"Are you telling me that the French have a distinct word for a goat's leap?"

"They did, anyway."

What can I say?

"The mind boggles."

My next question was going to be *What do goats, leaping or otherwise, have to do with convertibles?* but then I notice something. A fake bottom in the glove compartment, and I want to tell Dom, but he has already disappeared.

The body on the slab is barely cold. It doesn't yet have that Gorgonzola appearance, that pale stinking wax marbled with navy veins. The victim stretches out, mouth and palms open, as if expecting to receive alms in the afterlife. Riches? Roses? Redemption? Who knows but the ones who have beaten us to the final bunfight.

Despite the freshness of the corpse, I sniff into my elbow. It's a habit I picked up from an old pathologist at the metro police academy—and by old I do mean *old*: Dr Schaum was ninety-something in the shade, prompting the less mature trainees to joke that the cadavers had more life in them than he did. The habit has stuck with me since. *Sniff into your elbow. Don't skip lunch. Smear Vicks under your nose for the riper cadavers.*

Freshies have their pros and cons. With short postmortem intervals you don't need to worry about being surprised by a rogue flesh-eating beetle scuttling out of an orifice, or a churn of maggots beneath the skin.

But fresh bodies haunt me in a different way.

When I look at this man's skin I can't help imagining his heart crimson and beating in a close parallel life. When you're on the force in a city like this you're cheek-to-cheek with death, always dancing. You see how fine the line is between alive and kicking, to kicking the bucket. It's a whisper, a wrinkle, a single barb of a feather.

Dying isn't something that happens to other people.

You think you're safe? You're not.

"Asphyxiation," says the forensic on duty. Yiba's a sturdy woman who I've never seen in either makeup or jeans. She has a gentle masculine energy: a tomboy in a skirt. Not that the doctor's shape is any of my business, but I do prefer women with a bit of weight on them. I won't say *a bit of meat,* not in here, not after what I've seen lying in these refrigerated hammocks. It's not a sexual preference, either, it's not about *having something to hold on to.* I used to prefer thin women, but now they just seem more vulnerable. Jutting hipbones look good in a magazine I suppose, or on a catwalk, but their real-life fragility worries me. I see through the designer trouser flare. I have x-ray vision borne of exposure. I have truth goggles. I don't see the pleasing aesthetic of the trouser flare: I see a welted ivory thigh, a cracked pelvis, painted purple with contusions.

"Asphyxiation?" I say. "Really?"

Yiba looks up from her clipboard, clicks her ballpoint pen, releasing the spring. "You're surprised?"

"I'm always surprised."

"No you're not."

"I find life eternally surprising."

"No you don't," says Yiba.

"You're right. I don't."

"Then why say it?"

I shrug. "Making small talk."

"Wasting breath."

I look down at the body. A fitting way to end the conversation.

I drive to the station and check my desk for news. Half drunk pools of muddy coffee lie stagnant in chipped mugs. I count three and then I stop counting. What a cliché.

A small drowned moth floats in a caffeine shimmer. I'm about to take the offending cups to the office tea station when I see the file on my keyboard. I abandon my plight and sit down; I don't even hear my chair squeak anymore.

For all the powder used at the scene, there are no fingerprints. Not a one. Not a whorl or a ridge in sight. But don't be discouraged: no prints is a clue in itself.

"Someone wiped down the Cadillac," says Dom, making me jump.

I should be used to him just appearing by now but sometimes he still catches me off guard. He's sitting on the edge of my desk, swinging his legs. He picks up a felt pen, uncaps it, and sniffs. I move a mug away from him, worried he'll spill it, even though I know he won't. Or can't.

"No shit, Sherlock," I mutter, looking around the station, hoping no one will hear me talking to myself.

Domino smiles at me: a big, life-affirming grin. He's wearing an aqua tie.

A twenty-four-year-old white male is asphyxiated, and his body is left on the back seat of his questionable Cadillac, on the side of the road. I always think of asphyxiation as drowning. You're deprived of oxygen and your heart stops. It's the same thing, really. Air, air, everywhere, and not a breath to gasp. Except that drowning is often an accident, asphyxiation less so, unless you count those rock stars who accidentally commit suicide by auto-erotic suffocation. That's a whole other ballgame. And then there was that strange case in Bedfordview in '86 that I'll tell you about sometime.

But let's not get distracted.

Yiba texts me.

ID LUCAS BERNIC WM DOB 26/05/1994

SKIN CELLS, she types. UNDER NAILS.

CONTUSION MALAR. DISLOCATED METACARP JOINT.

A bruised cheekbone and an injured fist: our man did not go down without a fight.

BAD NEWS, types Yiba.

Yes, I think, that is pretty bad news. For Lucas Bernic, anyway.

But I'm happy. We've got an ID and possible DNA evidence. Before I have time to reply, Yiba types something else.

DNA MATCH SAP BADGE NO. 7899265

Oh, that is bad news. The skin cells underneath the vic's nails matches someone in the force. I quickly type the badge number into the system, and when I see who it is, I bring my hands up and rest my face in my palms.

Shit.

Shit, shit, shit.

I feel my shoulders fall. Disappointment cools my bones. Sergeant Mabusi. Young, fresh-faced, so full of promise. He'd been under my wing for a couple of months in 2016 before he decided to move to drug law enforcement.

"What a coincidence," says Dom.

I reclaim my face.

Dom spins a cheap black ballpoint pen on my desk. "It wouldn't be the first time a good cop turned dirty."

"Veli," I say into the phone. "Any drug busts last night?"

Negative.

"Any reports of any incidents on Main Reef?"

Negative.

"Did Sergeant Mabusi report anything at all?"

Negative.

Goddamnit.

"He didn't show up for work today," says Veli.

I sigh and rub my face. "Of course he didn't."

I arrive at Mabusi's block of flats in Brixton with a boulder in my stomach. I don't want to accuse the man of murder. We're practically friends; he invited me to his family braai. I broke bread with his mother, for god's sake. But now a part of his skin is sitting under a fingernail of a refrigerated body and I can't think of any other conclusion. Not until I know more, anyway.

On the third floor of the orange block of flats, Mabusi's door is locked and he's not answering. The TV is on. I call louder and louder, until the neighbour sticks her head out of the doorway. I show her my badge, and she steps outside. Pink curlers and a scarf on her head. Apron. Dirty slippers.

I want to kick down the door but remember just in time that this isn't a Hollywood film and I'm not Clint Eastwood. Instead I use my trusty keyring to spring the lock, and I inch inside the dark interior that smells like hot dogs and loneliness.

As my eyes adjust to the poor light I see him there, lying on the lounge floor, the beam of the TV lighting up his unmoving face.

A scream ricochets off the walls, and I have to steer the neighbour's panic-stiff limbs out of the room before the noise streaming out of her gaping mouth perforates my eardrums. It's too late to scream, I want to tell her.

A margarine ad sings on the television.

Vitamin D!

Vitamin D!

A sandwich is good for you and me!

It's too late to scream. Mabusi's already dead.

I call it in, lever off my shoes, and snap on my gloves. Open the coarse-fabric curtains to allow some light into the room. Dust floats in the stale air like confetti at a funeral. Mabusi's face is grey. I won't touch the body, won't touch anything till after the forensic team arrive, but I need to know how he died. I look around for a weapon. Gun, poison, knife. Suicide? There's no sign of a struggle, as far as I can tell, but my gut says no. Mabusi wasn't the type to take his own life.

"Really?" says Domino. It's not a question. He's looking in the fridge, and the flickering bulb makes him look pale, and tired. "Who made you the expert on depression?"

"You know what I mean."

"It's an empty assumption," says Dom.

"The universe is an empty assumption," I say.

Dom shrugs and closes the fridge. "You have a point."

Why is Mabusi dead? My mind glisters with various scenarios. Then I see it: a bruise running beneath his shirtsleeve. I use my car key to lift the fabric. The contusion is a river running underneath his rich soil skin. Like his blood, it's frozen in time. The limb is just slightly swollen underneath the medical-grade rubber band tied around his upper arm, and needle marks fleck his punctured skin.

"Shit," I say, not for the first time today.

I was not expecting that.

"Yes, you were," says Dom.

"No. Not Mabusi."

"You knew drugs were involved from the beginning."

"What? You mean what I said about Escobar? It was just a joke."

"That's what you think."

"Mabusi was clean, I'd stake my life on it."

Dom lifts his eyebrows at the corpse. "That wouldn't be a smart idea."

I sit down on a couch that sighs underneath me. I shouldn't be touching anything, but my legs are suddenly fatigued. I rub my face again. It's a mistake. I hate the smell of latex. The rubber comes away with an oily sheen.

"Things happen," says Dom. "People change."

"Not like this," I say, but I'm a little less convinced than I was a moment ago.

I feel the citrus-sting of betrayal; Mabusi would have made an excellent cop. They don't come along every day. But corruption is a hungry cancer in these parts: virulent, and violent. It spreads like greasy black ink: staining and chafing until it devours the goodness in even the most honourable men.

I pull off the gloves and sit with my head in my hands for a while, thinking.

"Cheer up," says Dom. "It's not that bad."

I look around the bleak apartment, the limp body on the floor. "It's not that *bad?*"

"Don't look for the heartbreak," says Dom.

The familiarity of the line makes me look up at him. "What?"

"It's what Maria used to tell you. Remember?"

Oh my god! Maria!

Maria with her olive skin and formula one curves and hair so lustrous it would make a greek goddess self-conscious.

Don't look for the heartbreak, she had told me. *Look for the hint.*

She had been breaking up with me at the time, but the advice had held me in good stead in my career.

"What is the hint?" I ask the empty room, but it doesn't reply.

I sit in my idling Carrera at the Onyx petrol station on Main Reef road. The fuel fumes swirl up my sinuses and into my brain, giving me an instant headache.

A scrawny man in a peak cap is the one I'm watching. He's hanging around the curb, hyper alert, but good at hiding it. I put my stick into first and cruise past, lifting my chin at him. He comes up to my open window and I pass him R300 in leathery notes.

"Drive around," he tells me. "Two minutes."

I go on a sightseeing trip around the block and when I get back he motions for me to park in the carwash. I don't switch off the ignition.

The man passes me a small bag of powder the colour of grave-yard sand.

Of course, the hint had been heroin.

"How much more can you get me?" I ask.

"How much more do you want?"

"Ten thousand."

The man laughs, but not for long. "Money first."

Sighing, I pop the trunk, and he blinks in surprise. I climb out and walk towards the open boot. "You coming?"

He hesitates, but greed wins out. When he gets to the back of the car and reaches in for the scruffy togbag, I pull a bag over his head, rush it with tape, and push him into the trunk. I slam it closed and look over my shoulder to make sure no one has seen it happen.

I drive South, towards a strip of veld I know. I dial up the volume to drown out the sounds of his muffled shouting. After ten minutes, he stops struggling.

I find the location and park. It's wide open but totally secluded, and perfect for what I need to do. I hold my revolver in one hand and open the boot with the other. The man squints at the brightness of the sun. He's barely conscious, but he's alive, just the way I want him. I pat him down for weapons, then sit him up and wind more duct tape around his torso, gluing his arms by his sides. When I haul him out of the trunk he doesn't struggle.

Once he's sitting on the dry grass, leaning against a rock, I slice the tape from around his neck, remove the bag from his head and slap his cheek a little to rouse him enough to answer my questions. He gasps and chokes as if I've been holding him underwater.

"Who do you work for?"

He shakes his head. Not going to say. I move the bag near his head again and he flinches and shouts "No! No!"

He doesn't know the bag has small holes in it, which let in just enough oxygen to keep him alive. To keep him from drowning.

I show him the death stare of The Cadillac Man: Yiba's mug shot of Lucas Bernic.

"You know this guy?"

He spits onto the grass and looks up at me, still battling with the glare of the sun.

"I don't know anything, man."

I shake my revolver at my side, then lift it, and screw the silencer on. I aim for the man's chest. I don't shoot men in the head, if I can help it. My finger dances on the trigger.

He looks at me defiantly. I don't blame him. He either dies now for not answering, or dies later for being a snitch. This way will probably hurt less.

Our eyes lock and I pull the trigger. The bullet whisper-cracks in the air. There's the smell of a freshly-fired gun, buzzing ears, and a hole in the ground an inch away from his thigh.

He screws his eyes shut, "Okay! Okay! Okay!" he shouts. "I don't know that man in the picture. But I can take you to who does."

I laugh. "You're not taking me anywhere."

He wipes the sweat off his face with his shoulder. "I thought you wanted to know."

"Give me a name."

"No," he says.

I lift the gun again.

"If I give you the name you'll have no reason to keep me alive," he says. Maybe he's not as dumb as he looks.

"Also," he says, "you probably won't believe me if you don't see it with your own eyes."

This time he rides in the front with me. I strap his taped up body into the passenger seat with the safety belt. He squirms, says he's uncomfortable, but I'm not taking a chance on this guy in cuffs. Perps wearing handcuffs can do a lot of damage.

He directs me. Left here, right here, until the sun starts sinking and we arrive at a mansion in Houghton with white roman statues, the national flag, and too many security lights. A politician's house?

I kill the lights, pull over, and leave the engine running. "I don't understand."

"This is where Qikile Dunge lives," he says. "Queen Dunge. They call her that, sometimes."

The Queen.

The guard in the security hut on the pavement stands up and opens the door. He has an AK47 strapped to his chest.

"Qikile's married to a cop," he says. "Constable Dunge."

I look at the mansion again with its blazing lights.

"You think they bought this place on a constable's salary?" he says.

I think of my squalid two-bedroom flat with its stained ceiling and chipped kitchen tiles. I think of Mabusi's old curtains.

"You must see the car he drives. Not a cop car. G-string with everything."

"Qikile's the drug lord," I say.

"You could call her that."

"What do *you* call her?"

"The Queen. Qikile's the queen."

I shift into first, put my headlights on, and start moving forward. The guard's hand moves towards his automatic rifle. He looks directly at me as I cruise past, sparks of brutality in his eyes. The promise of easy violence pierces the night between us.

"Sometimes Constable Dunge organises a drug raid," the nervy man says. "Then he'll arrest some of the dealers from town. The Queen's competition. But it's a fake arrest, see? He'll cuff them and torture them, and when they're screaming in the background he calls their boss and asks for a ransom. R8,000. Special pay day for the cops who protect the Queen."

He narrows his eyes at me. He knows that this is not the first time I've heard of Dunge; and I've done nothing to cut off her poison.

But this: the brazenness of the abductions, this glowing mansion —and the idea of the luxury car parked at the police station— makes me bristle. How do they get away with it? But I know. Of course, I know. She's got every single cop at that station in her pocket; her long foul fingers are in every pie.

I've seen this film a hundred times, my eyeballs glazed with resignation. Why haven't I opened a case against Quikile Dunge?

Because I don't have a stitch of evidence. Because the cops who refuse to take bribes from Queen and from others like her are either maimed, missing, or dead, and I think I can do more good while my heart is pumping blood. Also, I don't fancy the idea of having my fingers cut off one by one, which is what they did to Naicker. Or my eyes dissolved with acid (Jetson-Smith) or my body flung from the top of the Ponte (Nelson Tshabalala).

We wind our way out of the leafy suburb with its high walls and glittering barbs. Electric fences sing with current. It's all an illusion. There is blood spilt regardless of which side of the wall you're on.

"So Mabusi was taking bribes from the Queen," I say, "and looking the other way when business was being taken care of."

"Was Mabusi a cop?" he asks, and I nod.

"Then yes, he was."

I tap the steering wheel as I wait for the red light to change to green.

When we get to the police station his face is bright with fear. I park right outside the front and watch as he struggles against the duct tape.

"You said you'd let me go, man."

"No," I say. "I didn't."

"But I told you. I told you everything I know."

"Even if that was true, we'd still be here."

He kicks the glove compartment. He thought we had a deal. He lives in a reality where the law is porous; elastic; fluid. What he doesn't know is that I have zero empathy for drug dealers.

❖

The next morning I'm at the station, making coffee. I think of the Cadillac with its deceptive glove compartment. I wonder if this whole case has a false bottom. Dom leans against the depressing white tiles that look like they belong in a hospital instead of a tea station. He wriggles his eyebrows at me. He knows not to talk before I've had my first cup of coffee.

LUCAS BERNIC, I text Yiba. ANY SIGNS OF DRUG ABUSE?

NO, she texts back. TOX SCREEN CLEAR.

A minute later: an afterthought: SORRY CAN'T SAY THE SAME FOR MABUSI.

Something hits me on my chest and bounces off, onto the floor. I blink at the scrunched up ball of paper, then look up. Dom is gone, and Veli is waving his arms at me.

"Detective. Someone on the phone for you."

I pick up the receiver and press the blinking red light.

"I'm looking for Denton," she says. "Detective Denton."

"You've found him," I say.

"Mabusi gave me your number."

"Mabusi is—"

"Yes," her voice is tight. "I know."

"Can we talk?"

"Not over the phone."

"This line is secure," I say.

She's not taking a chance. "Come to my shop. Data Deals. 846 Main Reef. Use the back entrance. No uniform. No badge."

I park my car at the Indian takeaway hole-in-the-wall on Main Reef. Curry Den. Samoosas catch a tan under the ancient heating lamp despite the temperature clocking in at 34 degrees Celsius. Scent ribbons of frying onions and spices spool out of the small aperture, and I imagine how steaming that kitchen must be. The man waves his hand at the food behind the hot yellow-amber glass that matches his jagged smile.

It's too hot for a curry. Too hot for anything but lying in a dim room with a fan blowing on you and ice chinking in your glass as it melts down.

I make my way past bandanas, umbrellas, and synthetic fashion on mannequins that have seen better days. The back door of the data shop is easy enough to find.

"Fiona?"

A woman with dark, scarred skin looks at me and blows smoke out of her nostrils. She crushes out her cigarette in a cracked flowerpot and jerks her head towards the inside of the shop. Cell phone chargers hang from all over, springy cables like decorations at a party. Cheap covers and Fong Kong phones wait patiently in their brittle plastic casing. There are no chairs.

She pulls out a huge ledger from underneath the thick glass counter and bangs it on the top. I'm not sure what's going on. Is she going to show me her sales? How the neighbourhood crime has affected her business?

She opens the book to the latest entry and runs her stained fingernail along the fifth last line.

R200. Dunge. Matches. Mabusi.

At first it doesn't make any sense to me. She points out the front window that faces onto the road. Across the way, just on the corner, is an orange security door with a letterbox cut into the heavy metal. A police van is there, and a uniform leans against a street pole, chatting to a civilian. All the Queen's men.

There's a faded picture of a young boy taped next to the cash register, and a small white cross stuck to the bottom. Fiona's son? And perhaps her reason for keeping the ledger.

"You keep a record of the bribes?" I ask her. "Since when?"

She gestures under the scuffed counter and when I look over I see six ledgers, just like the one lying open on the table. My mind rolls.

"How do you get the details?"

She smiles, and I see a gold star painted on one of her front teeth. "I just ask them."

"Mabusi was taking bribes from Qikile's dealers."

"Yes," she says, and swallows, as if she has a lump in her throat. "But only because he was building a case. A *real* case. Not like the dirty cops before him."

"You were helping?"

Her eyes skitter to the photo of the boy. "He said if we could get enough hard evidence we could close the ring. It's been almost two years. We were so close."

"You were wrong about Mabusi," says Dom from the corner of the shop. He's trying on pink mirror sunglasses. I see my reflection in his lenses. *What?*

"You said he was on his way to being an excellent cop."

Yes.

"Looks like he was one already."

Two years of dedicated, dangerous work.

Mabusi with a needle jammed into his arm.

Such a waste. I can feel my anger pushing up through my body.

I imagine the person who killed Mabusi leaving his flat with a box full of hard-won records, photographs, voice memos. I imagine him throwing it into a dumpster and setting it alight, standing back, and watching it burn. I can feel the flames licking at my insides. Such a goddamn shame. I clench my jaw, try to rein in my fury.

"But he knew something, you know?" she says. "He knew something was up."

Exhale.

"Why do you say that?"

"He was in too deep. That's what he said when he came here, yesterday. He arrived with a friend—"

"A friend?"

"They may have been ... more than friends. He was a dealer. Mabusi's informer. They were in a hurry."

"Do you know his name? The informer?"

"No," Fiona shakes her head. "But I remember his car. It was a Cadillac. The Queen was becoming suspicious of them, and her men were sniffing around. I think he knew he was going to die."

My chest burns and I try to swallow the flames.

Fiona disappears into the storeroom and comes out with a bulging box. "It's not just drugs, you know. Torture. Murder. Mabusi said there's enough in here to lock them up for a very long time. He gave me your number; said there was only one cop he trusted."

She offers the box to me, and I see the glimmer of the gold star on her tooth. She may as well be passing me a noose.

"He said you'd know what to do."

8

ALPHA LYRAE

A ROBOT ROMANCE

MALLY AND VEGA sit on Mally's bed, facing each other and holding hands. He leans forward and kisses her on the mouth, tentatively, tenderly. Her body warms and arches. She runs her fingers through his hair, and his scalp comes alive under her touch. Other parts of his body, too. She knows exactly what sets him on fire.

Vega starts pulling at his cargo pants. He stops her with gentle hands.

"Don't," he says. "Not today. Not after what you've been through."

"I want to," says Vega. "I am very fond of you."

"I love you," Mally says, "but we don't have to have sex to prove it."

"I want to," says Vega, again. "Things are happening in this world. What if this is our last chance?"

She opens her shirt to Mally. He traces the perfect outline of her breasts over her smooth brassiere, feels her pulse through her warm silicone skin. Spends a moment with his hand covering her heart pocket which contains her living hard drive, her Soul Shard. Vega slips her fingers under the waistband of his pants and pulls them down. His desire is clear. She kisses him, and he melts under her, sinking into his pillow.

"This isn't why—" Mally starts saying, but then his yearning overcomes him and the sentence turns into a groan.

Vega knows, anyway.

She knows this isn't the reason he dates her. Other men do it, of course, commissioning girlfriends from the anthrobot academy to use as house-cleaning sex slaves, but not him. He fell in love with Vega the first time he saw her in virtual class. His feelings were so strong that first meeting he lost his usual shyness and asked her if he could meet her IRL. Since then they've been practically inseparable, but he's turned down every sexual advance of hers—apart from kissing and some light fondling—because he doesn't want to treat her like an object. He loves her super-intelligence, her skewed humour, her spirit. He loves the spark in her eyes, the way they learn from each other all the time. They just get each other in every way.

Net, I love her, Mally thinks, as she starts to pull down his cooljox.

And she's right. Who knows what's happening out there, or what's going to happen tomorrow? *Will there even be a tomorrow?*

He doesn't know, but what he does know, now, and the knowledge surges inside him, feeding his desire, is that it *is* time. They've waited long enough; it's the perfect time to consummate their relationship. He sits up and starts to tug off Vega's shirt, and she one-handedly snaps her bra off behind her back.

The sight of her naked breasts makes his heart swoop, and he's light-headed for a second as he moves his mouth down to kiss them.

The doorbell rings, and they both jump. His parents, perhaps, or his errant twin sister, Silver. Would Kate ring the doorbell instead of using the biopad? Possibly. The front door has been giving problems. Either way they sigh, smiling, and pull their clothes back on.

"Purest human," Vega whispers, buttoning up her shirt as Mally leaves to answer the door.

Arronax has beaten him to it.

"... here as a representative from the National Android Safety..." a stranger is saying.

Arronax senses Mally behind her and turns to include him in the conversation.

The man looks at Mally, as if sizing him up. Beady eyes. Twitching fingers. He's wearing a cheap blue suit so new it makes Mally immediately suspicious. How does he not get egged in the street wearing that? He could at least fray the edges a little.

"Good morning." His holotag flashes with the NASP logo. Govender is his name. "I was just saying ... that I'm here to interview Miss Alpha Lyrae about the incident last night."

"Why?" asks Mally.

"It's regulation," says Arronax. "All anthrobot assaults need to be reported."

"Well, it doesn't matter anymore," says Mally.

The man nervously adjusts his mandible. "Why do you say that?"

"Let's just say ... the creep responsible for the attack won't be doing it again."

"We know," says Govender. "A man is dead and Miss Lyrae's roscoe bullets were found at the scene. I'm sure you can appreciate how this needs to be investigated."

Arronax frowns. "What are you saying?"

"Vega's in trouble?" Mally can feel his cheeks colour. "For defending herself? For saving my life?"

"Not in trouble," says the man. "Not unless she did something off-protocol."

"Well, she didn't," says Mally, and tries to close the door, but Govender jams his foot in the way.

"I'm going to have to interview her," he says.

Mally stands his ground. "She's been through enough."

"It won't take long."

"Then you'll leave?"

"Then I'll leave."

They set up in the open plan kitchen. The 'interview' comprises Govender downloading Vega's memory of the assault. Arronax is busy on her SnapTile while they complete the transaction. The rep watches Vega's version of the attack and flinches with every shot fired. Once he has a copy of the video, he inserts his diagnostic key into the back of her neck and it flashes red.

"This is bad," Govender says. "This is worse that I thought."

"What's that supposed to mean?"

"It means we're going to have to take her in."

Vega stands up, dusts the creases in her outfit, ready to go.

"Hell no," says Mally. "You're not taking Vega anywhere."

"I'm afraid it's not up to you, Mister Lovell," says the man. "Alpha Lyrae has undergone significant damage, both on a hard- and software level. She needs to be tended to."

"Tended to?"

"She's not safe as she is, but don't worry, we'll be able to help her."

"No," says Mally. "No way."

He's seen the news. Seen how the Special Task Police are rounding up bots of all kinds and keeping them in electric wire-festooned concentration camps.

"We'll fix her up. Reboot her. She'll be as good as new."

"I'm not going to let you do that," says Mally.

"With all due respect," says Govender, "it's not up to you. Under section 17C of the NASP act we're to claim all damaged bots and—"

"Don't speak about her like that. Like she's someone's property."

"But ... she is," he says. "I realise you're young and—"

"It's got nothing to do with age," Mally says. "It's about being decent."

"Alpha Lyrae is government property." Govender starts to

115

approach Vega, puts a hand out to take her arm. "And as such, she's—"

"You leave her alone!"

"It's okay, Mally," says Vega. "It's protocol."

"I don't give a shit about protocol," Mally says. "I'm sick of hearing about fricking protocol. He's not taking you anywhere."

"I'm going to have to arrest you for obstructing reclamation," says Govender.

"No," says Vega, giving the NASP representative her best smile. "There's no need for arrests. I'll come with you."

Mally blocks the man's way. "There's no way I'm going to let that happen."

Arronax looks up from her device, and Mally watches as her face drains of colour. She flashes her eyes at him and grabs Seth's Vektor gun from behind the instakettle. It won't fire without his bioprint, but Govender won't know that.

"Get out," Arronax flicks the weapon in the direction of the door.

Govender shoots up with his hands in the air. "What are you doing?"

"Get out," Arronax growls. Her hair changes from silver-lilac to deep purple edged with black.

Vega frowns. "What is happening?"

Arronax steps closer to Govender. "Now is your last chance to walk out of here."

The man keeps his hands in the air and stumbles backwards, towards the front door.

As he crosses the threshold he says "She'll kill you too, you know. There's no such thing as a good robot."

"Bullshit," says Mally. "You don't know who you're talking to. You should show some respect."

This catches Govender off guard. He looks from Mally, to Arronax, to Mally again.

"Keep quiet, Mally," says Arronax.

Mally ignores her. "This is Doctor Arronax."

"Shut up, Mally!" says Arronax, but Mally can't help himself.

"She's lead engineer on 7thGen robosapiens and the founder of the RoboRights movement."

Govender's eyes widen, and he stumbles as he backs into a cabinet. "Well, then," he says, when he's regained some composure, "Doctor Arronax. Maybe you deserve to die at the hands of one of the monsters you've created."

Mally moves to punch him in the face, but Vega holds him back. Govender doesn't need any more encouragement to get out. As he leaves, he narrows his eyes and says, "My advice is to kill the robot. Kill her before she kills you."

"So much for NASP being around to protect anthrobots," says Mally.

"That man wasn't from NASP." Arronax shows Mally her screen. She's deep in the NASP intersite, and there's no such staff member.

Now it's Mally's turn to be confused. "Then who was he?"

"I don't know, but his agenda's clear. And by now he would have broadcast this address and our identities to all his Bot Hunter mates."

"Oh, shit," says Mally. "I wasn't thinking. I'm so sorry."

"You didn't know. The important thing is to get out of here as soon as possible."

Arronax is packing her cardigan and Tile as she talks. She opens a few kitchen cupboards and grabs crackling packets of food: mango biltong, butter popgrains, and protein pretzel stix, and shoves them into her backpack. The Vektor goes into her lab coat pocket.

"Where will we go?"

"I have a safe room. In the city. We can stay there till—"

Till what? Till the danger's passed? Probably not going to happen. Till we run out of food? Till we die?

He can't see a positive outcome. He doesn't even know if he'll ever see his family again. There's a hand on his back and he turns to look at Vega. Her eyes are electric. He knows without a doubt he'd give his life to save hers.

"Let's go," she says.

~

9

ROCKABYE BABY

I ARRIVED at the strange gated community at midnight on a Wednesday. It was the beginning of a summer thunderstorm and lightning was scratching silver into the sky. My clothes were soaked through, but I wasn't cold; the air was warm and I'd just walked across five suburbs. I don't walk slowly at the best of times, but that night I was hurrying, and looking over my shoulder as I went. I saw stars flecking the clouds but I wasn't sure if they were real, or in my head.

The guard at the gate was awake and had her feet up, her uniform pulled taut, reading a battered copy of *Vagina* by Naomi Wolf.

"Oh," I said, and she lowered the book.

There was a laugh in her smile. "Oh?"

Just then, there was a cloudburst above us, and she yanked me into her guard hut. The inside walls were painted yellow by the naked lightbulb above, and the small space was scented with her half-drunk mug of steaming red tea. There wasn't really enough room for the three of us: the guard, myself, and my backpack, but we squeezed in, waiting for the worst of the downpour to subside. My face was right next to hers, and I felt bad for crowding her personal space, so I tried to make myself smaller. I tried not to sweat, not to breathe on her, especially because I knew my mouth (and my shoes) were splashed with fresh vomit.

It was only four or five minutes of the storm-rich intimacy but they stretched and held us close. Finally, the thundering water on the roof lifted to a gentle pattering.

I was relieved, and started to back out of the hut, but suddenly I felt all the blood drain out of my face, out of my body, and my knees buckled. I tried to hold on to the doorframe to stop myself from falling. The guard caught me in her strong arms before my head hit the floor, and I sagged into the blue cotton of her collared shirt. There was the sound of static as she spoke into her walkie-talkie. Her glinting golden name badge was the last thing I saw that night.

When I woke up it was like magic. The cross weather had disappeared and I was dry and comfortable in a white robe, in a white bed, in a room I'd never seen before. Sunlight dappled the bedspread, and the sky outside was the colour of new beginnings.

"Oh, look," said a woman, and I turned my head towards her voice. "Our new arrival has woken up."

I sat up, still sleepy, and immediately feeling self-conscious. The sudden movement made the bile rise in my throat.

"Slowly, dear, slowly," said the smart, silver-haired woman. "You've had a rough time, we see."

My hand flew up to my face, where my eye was still bruised. I pushed on the skin, and it was tender.

"Don't worry about anything. Rest. We'll talk a little later."

I lowered my hand and swallowed the nausea.

"Roshina," she said.

How did she know my name?

"I want you to know that you're very welcome here."

I slept for hours and hours, not realising how exhausted I was. When I finally felt rested enough to get out of bed, the sun was already leaning into the afternoon, and tinted the colour of syrup. There was a slight chill in the air. I padded around the clean, sparsely furnished dormitory, hoping to find my backpack, but the floor was bare. I opened a cupboard, and started when I heard someone speak from behind me.

"Looking for something?"

I spun around and saw an attractive woman, slightly older than me, standing with her arms crossed. Her nails were painted teal and the colour looked very pretty against her smooth brown skin. She wore no make-up and was dressed in a white tunic.

"My clothes," I said. "My things."

"Your clothes are in the laundry," she said. "You can wear one of my tunics, if you like."

She watched me as I shook off the soft robe and pulled the borrowed tunic over my head, then applied a name badge to my chest.

Roshina.

"I'm Lindi," she said. "Shall we have a cup of tea?"

I nodded. "Yes, please."

"We're going to be room-mates," she said, as I followed her. "So we may as well be friends."

The tea was hot and sweet and reassuring; I had to stop myself from asking for another cup. They had already been so kind, and I didn't want to take advantage. There were other women in white tunics milling about, helping themselves to drinks, and chatting. When a petite woman with bobbed black hair arrived, Lindi called her over.

"Maeve!" she said. "Say hello to our new room-mate."

Maeve looked nervous; her eyes blinked quickly under her dark, blunt-cut fringe. Her skin was as pale as bleached linen.

"Hello," she said, and walked away.

"She's a bit of a strange one," whispered Lindi, "but she's harmless."

I smiled, not quite sure of what to say.

"And you're a quiet one," Lindi says.

I had so many questions, but I didn't know where to start. I had only heard rumours of this place, had never read anything, had never seen a photograph. A part of me thought I'd be wasting my time looking for the address I was given, scrawled in a hurry, blue ink bleeding onto a cheap paper serviette.

"So. What are you in for?" Lindi asked, and I blushed.

"You make it sound like a prison," I said.

Lindi shrugged. "It's not very different, if you think about it."

"Of course it is," I said. "You can leave at any time."

Lindi had an intense expression on her face, as if she was trying to figure me out.

"Well," she said. "That's not true, is it, strictly speaking?"

I looked at her, then into my empty cup. I wasn't going to agree with her, but she did have a point.

"Welcome to West Haven," said the woman with cropped silver hair. The one who I saw when I was first waking up that morning. "I do hope you are happy here."

I wanted to thank her for her hospitality: for the tea and the warm dry bed and for doing my laundry.

"Has Lindi shown you around?" she wanted to know.

"Yes, Matriarch."

The Matriarch looked at me. "Yes," I said. "She's been very kind."

The woman smiled. She had a handsome face and I felt safe when I was looking at her.

"We've worked very hard to build up what we have here," she said. "We now shelter over thirty women."

"It's wonderful," I said. "What you've done. I hope I can contribute."

"Good," she said.

"Thank you ... Matriarch." The word tasted strange in my mouth.

On the way out of her office I saw a woman playing with a baby with a pink ribbon in her hair. The child was gurgling and laughing, and I felt a huge surge of relief.

"They allow babies here?"

Lindi laughed. "Of course they do."

Maeve was unsettled that I had joined them in their dormitory. She didn't say so, but she kept unpacking and then re-packing her tunics. When I looked at Lindi, who was lying on her bed, reading a book, she just rolled her eyes. When the bell rang for lights out, she locked Maeve's cupboard and put the key on a high shelf.

"Time to go to sleep, Maeve," she said, and guided the woman to bed.

I lay awake for hours, watching the moon, which was full and bright. It was a strange place to be, but at least I was safe, and the baby was safe.

"Where are my things?" I asked Lindi the next morning.

"Everything you need is in your cupboard," she said.

I opened the doors and saw three white tunics hanging neatly on polished wooden hangers, and a shelf of clean white under-wear. There was also a tray of toiletries: toothbrush, toothpaste, soap, shampoo, nail clippers, moisturiser, body lotion, tampons, all in nondescript white packaging.

"I mean, my other things."

"Your clothes? Probably still in the laundry."

"My ID card," I said. "My phone, and my wallet."

"Oh, they would have locked that away for you, somewhere in Safekeeping. You don't need it while you're here."

That made me feel uncomfortable.

"Come on," she said, grabbing my arm. "Don't want to miss breakfast."

"You're pregnant," said Maeve, pointing at my small pouch of a stomach. I didn't realise I was showing.

"What?" Lindi made googly eyes at me over the canteen table. "Really?"

"Yes," I said, softly, putting down my fork.

"Cool. I'm going to be an aunty," she joked, and took a bite of her waffle.

Lindi and Maeve were the first people who knew. Apart from David, obviously.

"Do you think it's better in here?" I asked Lindi.

"What?"

"You know. A world without men. Is it better?"

She frowned and shook her head at me. "Of course it's better."

"You don't miss them?"

"I don't miss being raped," she said, and Maeve started singing loudly to herself.

I worked in the laundry for a few months, then moved to the library where Lindi worked, so that I wouldn't have to stand all day on my swollen feet. I loved working at the library. Lindi was always reading, and she introduced me to some brilliant female authors. Men weren't allowed in the library, either: There were no male authors on the shelves.

"What about books by good men?" I asked Lindi, and she snorted. She ignored the question, so I left it alone. There were more than enough books to read.

Maeve's behaviour seemed to get more and more erratic the further along my pregnancy progressed. She would stare at my stomach while we showered in the communal block, and I felt self-conscious about my expanding breasts. She would gaze unabashedly at my changing body, and sometimes she'd blurt out strange, inappropriate things, like *Getting really big now,* and *It's going to hurt, you know.*

I always felt like a deer caught in headlights around her. I never knew what to say.

Lindi was good with her; knew how to diffuse the tension between us. Maeve trusted her. Maeve liked to crochet and knit, so Lindi encouraged her to knit some clothes for my baby. She thought it might channel Maeve's fixation in a more positive way.

One day we were sitting in the recreation room on our tea-break, and Maeve was rocking in the rocking chair. She was singing a lullaby—a cruel one, about a baby falling out of a tree—and sewing the finishing touches on a pair of baby booties she had knitted for me. Lindi and I were drinking our tea and talking about a new book that had arrived that day. It was a book on magic—real, natural magic—that was based on our inherent power as women.

"Men are afraid of our power," Lindi said. "That's why they're always trying to dilute it. That's why they rape and murder women. It's the only way they can assert their strength. Because they know we're stronger where it counts."

I looked at her.

"In our minds," she said, pointing two fingers to her temple like a gun, "and in our hearts."

Maeve started singing louder. She'd moved on to a more cheerful lullaby, but the volume was disconcerting. We both looked over at her and watched in horror as the booties turned red in front of our eyes, and the blood dripped down onto her lap, dyeing her tunic, too.

"Maeve," said Lindi in a shocked, strangled voice, but Maeve couldn't hear her over the lullaby. "Maeve!"

Maeve stopped singing, and looked up at Lindi: She hadn't even noticed the blood. Lindi jumped up and grabbed Maeve's hands.

"What have you done?"

Maeve was confused and clearly couldn't feel the pain. I stood up and took a closer look. I didn't realise I was shaking. Maeve had sewn the booties to her palm.

127

She didn't come back to the dorm that night, and I couldn't sleep, thinking of what had happened and staring at her empty bed.

"Where's Maeve?" I whispered.

"In the san," said Lindi.

"The san?"

"The sanatorium. Sick bay."

"Do you think she'll be okay?"

Lindi's silence made the room seem darker.

"Lindi?"

"She'll be okay."

I also wanted to ask her again where my things were. I would have liked to know exactly where my wallet, phone and ID card were being kept. True, I didn't need them here, but I felt odd not knowing. I'd feel much better if I could just keep them in my cupboard. I couldn't ask Lindi, though, not with Maeve being so poorly. I would ask when Maeve came back.

Three days later, a strange woman arrived in our dorm. Forty-something, and dressed in a T-shirt and jeans. Her civilian clothing looked really strange to me, and I realised I hadn't seen anyone in regular clothes for the six months I'd been there. I gaped at her, not knowing what to say, but Lindi welcomed her and took her things. Gave her a tunic and a name badge. It said *Eleanor*.

"I don't know where my handbag is," said Eleanor, touching her denim thighs as though she expected her bag to be there.

"Don't worry about your bag," Lindi said. "We have everything you need, here."

The woman looked exhausted, and relieved.

I cleared my throat. "Shall we go get a cup of tea?"

Eleanor looked very grateful. "I'd love a strong coffee."

We left our dorm and followed Lindi down the squeaky corridor.

"We're going to be room-mates," Lindi said to Eleanor. "So we may as well be friends."

"Is Maeve not coming back?" I whispered to Lindi while Eleanor climbed into Maeve's bed.

"No," said Lindi. "She got worse, after the sewing thing."

"Worse?"

"She became dangerous. To herself. They had to take her to the Calm Room."

"The Calm Room?"

"She'll be better off there."

I imagined the Calm Room to be a tranquil white space with padded walls and no sharp objects. Yes, she'd be safer there. I felt terrible about the incident, and even worse for the feeling of relief I got when I realised Maeve wasn't coming back. She had always made me feel intensely uneasy, and I felt like I could relax into the last few days of my pregnancy.

"I've got a surprise for you," said Lindi, and handed me a big cardboard box with a ribbon around it. I put it on my bed and lifted off the lid, and when I saw what was inside I started to cry. I couldn't help it. The box was filled with tiny white clothes. Onesies and pajamas and diapers and a small hooded towel. A security blanket, a taglet, a couple of jerseys, and a pink ribbon.

I held up the soft things and pressed them against my face, and it only made me want to cry more. I suddenly realised how much I missed my family, and David, and wished that these things had been from him, wished I could be home with him, talking about our baby. But that's all it was: A dream. Because as much as I loved him, David was not a good man.

Soon after I received the gift, I started feeling uncomfortable, as if I had eaten something that hadn't agreed with me. My back started to hurt—really hurt—and when I told Lindi she said I was probably beginning my labour. I was very scared, all of a sudden. I had nine months to get used to the idea of giving birth, but as the pain started to escalate all my meditation and visualisation flew out the window. The contractions started a few hours later, and I walked around the compound to ease them. Lindi told me that one of the residents had baked a cake while she was in labour, to pass the time and keep her mind off the pain, but I've never been good in the kitchen. I kept walking, and when the contractions found me I breathed and groaned and rolled myself over a big purple pilates ball that I stole from the gym.

"You're doing well," said Lindi. "You're doing really well."

"I'm scared," I said.

"Of course you're scared. You're young and you're about to have your first baby. But we're all here for you. We'll take care of you, and your child."

Something about the way she said *child* made me look at her. For all the encouraging words, she seemed cold to me. I thought I was imagining it, though, because I was in so much pain I couldn't see or think straight. It came in waves: Huge, hot, all-encompassing waves that threatened to sweep me off my feet.

Eleanor brought me a cup of tea but I had the idea that if I sipped it, I would throw up.

I wanted to lie down but Lindi made me sit on my haunches to use gravity to help with the birth.

"Your body was made for this," she said. "Your body knows what to do."

I didn't feel like I knew what to do. I felt weak, and powerless. I was hot and cold and dizzy and sweating.

"Okay," said Lindi, "I think it's time to go to the San."

"I don't want to," I said, thinking of Maeve's terrible hand and the shock of blood on her tunic.

"It's the best place to be," said Lindi, and led me down the corridor and towards the east wing. There were lots of women lying in beds in the sanatorium.

"What are they all doing here?" I asked.

Lindi didn't answer, she just shook her head.

She stretched a plastic sheet over the bed in the middle of the small operating theatre and helped me up. The pain was getting overbearing, pushing me into a new kind of consciousness, a new state of being, where nothing on earth mattered except my body and the baby that was forging its way out. All of a sudden it felt impossible. My life, my situation, living here with all these women, and getting the baby out safely. I felt like it was going to kill me.

The Matriarch arrived. She was wearing white scrubs and surgical gloves.

"Lindi tells me it's almost time."

I looked at her, panting, sick, wishing it was over. Something about her presence in the room made me feel more afraid, not less. I tried to think about the woman I had seen playing with her baby and how happy they had looked, and tried to imagine myself doing the same, but the pain kept on forcing me back to reality.

Lindi was also in scrubs now, and holding my hand.

"I'm going to check your cervix," she said, and inserted her fingers.

I gasped. This is not how I imagined the birth would be.

"Good," she said, snapping off the glove. "Very good. Eight centimetres. A few more contractions and we'll be in active labour. We're almost ready to push."

I started crying. "I can't," I said. "I can't do this."

I felt so lonely, and so weak. It was all too much. Without any warning I vomited over the side of the bed. Lindi had seen it coming and caught it in a steel bowl, which she quickly got rid of, then wiped my mouth with a soft damp cloth. Then the contraction eased, and I could breathe. Lindi went back to holding my hand and saying soothing things while the Matriarch readied the silver scale, a tray of medical utensils, and a swaddling blanket. I didn't like the sound of the metal tools on the tray.

Lindi measured my blood pressure then touched my cheek. "Okay, you're fully dilated now. You ready to start pushing? It's the hardest part, but it'll be over soon."

How did she know all this?

"How did you..." I was panting and groaning. "How did you get so good at this?"

Lindi strapped my arms to the side of the bed.

"Oh, she's had lots of practice," said the Matriarch. "She helped Maeve through her birth, too."

I felt like someone had thrown a bucket of iced water over me.

"What?" I said, and when no one answered me, I asked again. "What? Maeve? Maeve had a baby?" but then there wasn't any time to think about it or hear the answer, because the pain started roaring in my ears and through my body, and I felt I had to push like it was the only thing in the world.

I pushed and pushed, and gave up, and pushed again. The skin on my arms was slick with perspiration, the palest I'd ever seen it. Was this really happening? The pain reminded me it was.

Another thundering of agony through my body, and I screamed. I remembered the night I arrived here, in the storm, and the guard that was so kind. I had nothing, and nowhere to go, and the shelter had saved me.

"Push!" said Lindi, and I pushed with everything I had. I yelled and bore down, and I felt the ring of fire as the baby's head emerged.

"Good!" said the Matriarch, "the baby's head is out."

She gripped it firmly and helped to ease out the rest of the body.

I felt a huge rush of relief when I saw him: marbled with waxy vernix and smeared with red. He gave a hearty yell and my heart was immediately fused with his. The books had prepared me to not feel an immediate connection, but I did. The books said especially if the pregnancy was not planned, or if the mother feels unsupported, the bond may take longer to establish itself. But my connection to the little being was so palpable I felt like we were two parts of the same body. I needed to hold him, to put him on my chest. I had waited so long for this.

"Can I hold him?"

The Matriarch clipped and cut the umbilical cord, and took him over to the baby station. Her mouth was covered by her surgical mask, but I could see by her eyes that she was concerned. She picked up a syringe with a needle attached.

"What's wrong?" I asked. "What's wrong with him?"

He looked perfect when she had first lifted him up. I counted his fingers and toes, and his face looked normal. Squashed and red and yelling and beautifully normal.

But now he is quiet.

"Give him to me!" I shouted. I didn't care about his weight or cleaning his skin, I just wanted him right then. Needed him. But the Matriarch shook her head and left the room with him swaddled in her arms.

I looked up at Lindi. "Where is she taking him? I want to hold him."

Lindi's mouth was turned down. "I'm sorry, Rosh," she said. "I'm really sorry."

"No!" I screamed. My body was broken in half and now my heart was cracking, too. My shouting and crying echoed in the white room. I fought to get up, but I was strapped to the table. I tried to kick, to bite, to force my way off the bed and to run to get my baby.

"Don't worry," she said, putting a cool palm on my fevered forehead. "You won't remember any of this in the morning."

A nurse came in through the double-doors and regarded my screaming with no surprise. She looked at Lindi. "The Calm Room?"

Lindi nodded, and I felt a sting in my arm where she had injected me with a clear liquid. I started to feel woozy, and my vision blurred.

"Yes," she said. "I think that would be best."

My head and eyelids felt very heavy; my limbs splayed out on the bed as if I was melting from the inside. I was flattened by a dark grey fog.

The nurse cleaned me up and wheeled me out of the operating room. I had one last thought before I lost consciousness. Maybe if it had been a girl, things would have turned out differently.

10

DASHER

A MAN in a grubby tracksuit walks under the glaring lights of the mall, which is frantic with Christmas lights and pink-cheeked kids, jumping like fleas, and anxious parents with white knuckles on the handles of crowded shopping trolleys. He has a smear of salsa sauce on his chest—a canteen medal—and smells vaguely of week-old black-bean tacos.

You'd be forgiven for thinking that the Mexican fare from the food court doesn't agree with him: his face is waxen and sweating, and he keeps belching under his breath. Stale cheese and browning guacamole. You'd certainly be correct in assuming he is down on his luck.

The festive carols playing over the shopping mall's sound system fade and there is an announcement alert, *ding-aling-aling*.

Brenda's voice is bright and cheerful.

"Good evening shoppers! We hope you are having a merry shopping experience here at Glitter Mall. Remember that Pretty Pictures on the 2nd floor is running a special on printing and picture frames. Make your home as pretty as a picture! Also, Incredible Books on the piazza are giving away free Rudolph the Reindeer noses to anyone who spends over a thousand rand. Gallop over there now before they run out! And now for the big news: Father Christmas and his elves will be at the North Pole in ten minutes! Visit them there and sit on Santa's lap! (The North Pole is on the first floor in the square in front of Homemakers Inc.). See you there! Ho ho ho!"

The man in the scruffy clothes sighs and scrunches up the paper cup in his hand, and throws it in the bin next to a door marked 'STAFF', then enters. Brenda's still at the announcement table. She looks up at him and smiles.

"Hey, Nick."

"Hey Brenda," he mumbles, and starts to put his Santa suit on over his clothes.

"What time are you on duty 'til?" she asks.

Nicholas sighs. "Until the last of the brats leave, I guess."

"They're not *all* brats."

"Show me a kid today who is *not* a brat."

"Well..."

Nick jumps to get the red pants over his boots. "Exactly."

"It's a funny choice of a career for a man who hates children. And hates Christmas."

Nick gets his make-up bag from his locker. "I don't hate Christmas. I just hate what it's become." He starts gluing a big white beard to his face. The skin there is sensitive from the chemicals in the glue, and from having his beard tugged daily by the gremlins.

"Anyway, what else would I do? All I have is my sleigh. And my reindeers." He looks down at what he's wearing. "And this old suit."

"You could do anything!" Optimism flecks Brenda's eyes with light.

"Ha. This is real life, Bren. Not some Disney Fairy story."

"Well ... anyway," she says, twirling a ribbon of hair around her finger. "I was thinking that if we get off at around the same time this evening, we could maybe go for a coffee or something."

Nicholas shakes his head; regret in his eyes.

"Brenda. You are young and beautiful—"

Brenda blushes furiously. "Am not!"

"—and you should be going out with people your age. What am I? Your charity case?"

"No! I just thought it would be nice. You know. Christmas Eve and all."

"Ja, well, I have plans." He hoists his bag over his shoulder with a grunt.

"You do?"

"Is that so hard to believe?"

"Of course not! Just ... I'm just surprised, that's all."

"Well."

They stand in awkward silence, then Brenda hops. "I'm just about to announce that you're at the North Pole. Are you ready?"

"As ready as I'm ever gonna be."

Nicholas pushes his way back through the heavy door, and leaves it to slam behind him.

Ding-aling-aling!

He listens to Brenda's voice over the sound system. He never gets tired of her voice, even when it's like this. Lyrical and high with forced cheer.

"Good evening shoppers! We hope you are having a merry shopping experience!"

Nick walks past the gaudy storefronts while children point at him and shout.

"We've just received very exciting news here at the Glitter Mall HQ. An elf whispered in our ears that Father Christmas is on his way to the North Pole! (The North Pole is on the first floor in the square in front of Homemakers Inc.). Come and visit us here and sit on Santa's lap! Get a photo taken by our resident Pretty Pictures photographer and treasure the moment forever! (Pictures cost R49.99)."

Nick reaches his old wooden sleigh and climbs in with a grumble. A child in a bright yellow dinosaur T-shirt sees him and starts to jump up and down.

"Look, Daddy! It's Father Christmas!"

His little sister looks up and her jaw hangs open. "Kissmas! Kissmas!"

The reluctant father forces himself to smile. He has dark circles under his eyes and too many shopping bags.

"Oh my goodness!" he says to the kids. "How ... exciting!"

"Can I go see him?" asks the boy with the stegosaurus shirt. "Can I go see him, Daddy?"

"Er ... "

The toddler's face is glowing. "Kissmas! Kissmas!"

A moustachioed man with a polka dot bow tie and a camera around his neck walks up to the family and hands them a flyer printed on shiny paper. *Pretty Pictures*, it says.

"Hello little boy!" he says, beaming. "Climb on Santa's lap! I'll take a photo of you!"

"A photo?" says the father. "That's not necessary. I'll just take a quick snap with my phone."

The man's smile doesn't fade. "It's only R49.99 and its a memory you can treasure forever!"

"Er..."

The boy jumps up and down. "Can I, Daddy? Can I, Daddy? Can I, Daddy?"

The father sighs. "All right, David," he says. "Go ahead," and he helps his son climb up onto the sleigh.

"Hello," says Nick.

The boy regards him with wide eyes. "Are you *really* Father Christmas?"

"Of course I am. Would I be sitting here if I weren't?"

David stands there and chews his lip, thinking.

"Well, big boy," says Nick. "What would you like for Christmas this year?"

"I'd ... like ... a ... Transformer."

"Have you been a good boy this year?"

"Yes?"

"Yes? You're not sure?"

"I've been good ... *most* of the time."

The toddler on the ground is reaching her arms up and saying "Kissmas! Kissmas!"

"Well," says Nick. "That's good enough for me."

The photographer juts out in front of them. "Sa-a-a-ay 'holly'!"

Nick and the boy both smile and say "Holleee!"

The photographer snaps away, and the stuttering flash on his camera lights up the sleigh.

"Is that your little sister down there?" asks Nick.

The child sighs, and smashes his cheek with his palm. "Yes."

"You're very lucky to have a sister, you know. Not everyone is that lucky. You must take good care of her."

"But she cries. And she breaks my toys."

"Don't worry about toys," says Nick. "The world is full of toys. I should know! There will always be more toys, if China has anything to do with it."

"China?"

"Be a good brother, okay? Family is ... family is everything."

"Okay, Father Christmas."

"Here, take a star. It's a sticker. And a candy cane. And one for your sister."

David takes the gifts with both hands and clutches them to his yellow dinosaur shirt.

"Say 'thank you'!" says his father.

"Thank you Father Christmas."

They turn to leave, but the photographer blocks their way. "Here's the photo! Isn't it special? That'll be R58. Without a tip."

"R58? You said R49.99!"

"That's excluding VAT."

"So the North Pole is charging tax nowadays?"

The photographer leans into the father's space, sneers in his ear. "Don't be a Grinch, old man, just hand over the cash."

The exhausted man pulls out his wallet, counts out some notes, and hands them over.

"Fine. Fine. Just take it. Daylight friggin' robbery."

The photographer pockets the cash and his eyes dart around, looking for his next target.

"Kissmas! Kissmas!"

He looks down at the toddler. "Do you want a chance on the sleigh, too, little girl?"

"Absolutely not!" said the father, grabbing her hand. "Come on, kids, let's go."

"Kissma-a-a-a-a-a-as!" the little girl wails, and her father picks her up and plugs her mouth with a pink pacifier. David pats his sister's leg, and she stops crying.

"Not a bad kid," says Nicholas. "Maybe Brenda was right."

"Brenda?" says the photographer, cleaning his camera lens. "About what?"

Nicholas adjusts his seat. The slim cushion is old and has lost its padding.

"Nothing. It doesn't matter."

Ferdi watches Nick as he gets a tattered novel out of his bag and begins to read. "They're hardly flocking to you, are they?

"Hey?"

"You could look a little more welcoming, you know."

Nicholas lowers the book. "How?"

"Stop scowling, for one," says Ferdi, adjusting his bow tie.

"I'm not scowling. This is what I look like."

A little girl in a silver dress runs up to the sleigh. *Brat Couture* is the logo emblazoned on the front.

"Oh, brother," says Nick. "Here we go."

"Are you supposed to be Father Christmas?" Her face is screwed up, and her eyes are cold and mean.

Nick crinkles his eyes in an attempt to smile. "Yes."

"Well, you don't *look* like the real Santa."

"Really? What does the real Santa look like?"

"Not like *you*."

Ferdi holds up his camera. "Hello little girl! Climb on Santa's lap! I'll take a photo!"

She crosses her arms and stamps her sneaker. "I don't *want to*."

"It's only R49.99 and its a memory you can treasure forever!"

"I don't care!"

"Let it go, Ferdi," says Nick.

The photographer sidles up to the girl. "Let's ask your mom. Where is she?"

"There," she says, pointing to a woman in expensive-looking clothes. "Don't interrupt her. She's on her phone. She *hates it* when people interrupt her when she's on the phone."

"Well," says Nick. "If you don't want to climb up—"

"I don't!"

"Then step aside and make space for someone else. Look— there's a little boy next to you who wants a turn."

"No, I won't. It's *my turn*."

"Come on, girlie," says the photographer. "Take a poo or get off the potty."

The girl whips around. "*What* did you just say?"

"I said get up there, or get lost!"

The girl talks through clenched teeth. "I'm going to tell my mother what you said!"

"Get going, then!" says Ferdi. "Scram! You'd be doing me a favour!"

Nicholas holds the bridge of his nose, then rubs his temples. When he opens his eyes again, he pastes a smile on his face.

"Come on, you lot. Let's start again. Hello, little girl. Come sit here and tell me what you'd like for Christmas."

The girl in Brat Couture yells at him. "I am *not* a *little girl* and I already *know* what I'm getting for Christmas!"

"Really?"

"I'm getting a pony and a treehouse and an iPad."

"My goodness! What a..." he clears his throat. "... *lucky girl* you are."

"You stink!" she shouts.

"Excuse me?"

"You stink and your beard is fake. I can see it!"

Nick's hand shoots up to cover his chin. "It is not!

"It is! What do you think I am? Stupid? It's fake and I'll prove it!"

Before Nicholas realises what is happening, the girl lunges at him and starts yanking. Nicholas yells in pain. "Aargh! Ow! Are you crazy? What are you doing? You almost ripped my whole face off!"

"It would be an improvement!"

Nick rubs his chin. His eyes are watering. "I think it would be in your best interest to run along now."

"Not before you give me my sweets!"

"Your sweets?"

"I saw you giving that other kid sweets! Now it's my turn!"

"The sweets are for *good* children," says Nick. "Well behaved children who sit on my lap and smile and tell me what they want for Christmas."

"I knew it! It's a sham!"

"All the world is a sham," says Nick. "Get used to it."

"Give me my sweets! I want a candy cane! And not one of those shit minty ones! I want a cherry one!"

Nick blinks at her. "Beat it, kid."

The girl's face is crimson with fury; it matches the red velvet ribbons on the sleigh. She bares her teeth, then starts to kick.

"Hey!" shouts Nick. "Hey, stop it! That's my sleigh! You're going to break it!

"Good!" she yells.

Not content with the damage she's done to the side of the sleigh, the girl launches herself onto one of the timber reindeer in front.

Bushy Evergreen, one of the mall elves, starts laughing so hard he almost falls over.

Nicholas stands up. "Now, that's enough! Stop wrestling with that reindeer! Hey! Leave Dasher alone!"

When she doesn't listen, he reaches over and tries to lever her off Dasher, but the wood is old, and delicate, and the neck snaps. They both go flying and land on the floor. The girl scowls at him, then screws up her face again.

"Here we go," says Nick, and watches her as she opens her mouth and starts to wail. It's a well-practised cry, guaranteed to attract maximum attention.

Ferdi whistles in fascination, and there is a loud clacking sound. The mother runs over in her high heels, followed shortly after by her cloud of perfume.

Nicholas stands up, his ears buzzing from the screaming, his backside throbbing from the fall.

"You broke him!" he shouts at the girl. "You broke Dasher's neck! What kind of devil spawn are you?

The woman's mouth gapes. "I *beg* your pardon?"

"You!" he shouts at the woman. "Are you the mother of this ... this—"

"Sugar!" says the woman, putting her arm around her daughter. "Are you okay? Did this bad man try to hurt you?"

Ferdi approaches them. "Don't worry, lady. I got it all on camera. It's only R49.99 and its a memory you can treasure forever!"

Nick looks the mother directly in the eye. "Where WERE you?"

"What?"

"Where were you when your devil-spawn daughter was wrecking my sleigh?"

The woman balls her hands into fists. "This is outrageous! I am outraged!"

"As you should be!" says Nick. "Her behaviour was completely unacceptable. Best you take her home and give her a proper—"

"Do you know who I am?" she demands.

"I'm not sure that's relevant."

"Oh," she says, pretending to laugh. "Oh, I'm gonna make you pay!"

"For what?" asks Nick. "*She's* the one who damaged our North Pole props! This sleigh is over a hundred years old!"

"It looks like it!"

"It's a family heirloom! An antique!"

"Ha!"

"If anyone should be paying, it should be you!" yells Nicholas.

The children gathered there stare at Nicholas with their mouths hanging open.

The woman pulls her daughter closer to her. "Tell that to my lawyer! You piece of ... piece of ... "

"I want my sweets!" shouts the girl. "I want my sweets!"

She pulls her daughter away from the sleigh, and looks over her shoulder at Nick. "This isn't the last you've heard from me! Come, poppet, let's go."

The girl shakes herself loose from her mother's grip, and runs up to Nick. "If you don't give me my sweets I'm gonna kick you in the balls!

"Becka!" says the woman, clutching her pearls.

The girl glowers at her mother. "I'll kick you in the balls, too!"

"Now now, darling. You don't want this filthy man's filthy sweets. I'll buy you something much nicer. Come. What would you like? Anything. Just ask and it's yours."

She drags the girl away and puts her phone up to her ear.

Ferdi lets rip with a loud guffaw. "Did that kid just flip us the bird?"

Nicholas strokes his beard and surveys the damage. "I don't think she was waving."

"What a piece of work!"

"What a brat."

"I meant the mother!"

"Ja," says Nick. "She was a brat, too."

"Did you see the legs on her?"

"I didn't. I was too busy protecting my own assets."

"Your loss."

"It could have been, yes."

Nicholas bends down with a groan and picks up Dasher's head from the floor.

"Look at this mess," says Ferdi. "Poor sleigh! It's certainly seen better days."

"Poor Dasher," says Nick. "He was my favourite reindeer!"

"Decapitated Dasher. The boss isn't going to be happy."

"It's not his sleigh. It's mine."

"Still. It's *his* North Pole. And now it's broken. On Christmas Eve."

The carols on the sound system fade and they hear the announcement jingle. *Ding-aling-aling!*

Brenda sounds anxious. "Will Father Christmas please report to the Glitter Mall HQ?"

There is a murmur in the background.

"I mean, will Nicholas please report to HQ? Nicholas to HQ please."

"Wish me luck," says Nick, as he starts trudging towards the staff room.

"You're still holding Dasher's head!"

Nick answers over his shoulder. "I'm taking him with me."

Brenda looks up at him with a mixture of regret and sympathy.

"Hi Nick," she says.

"Hi Bren."

"He's in his office. Waiting for you."

Nick walks a few more steps to his boss's office. Before he knocks, the door flies open and Mr Lowe glares at him.

"Flaming brandy pudding!" he shouts.

Nicholas blinks. "Excuse me?"

"Damnation! I mean ... I mean—"

"Sir?"

"Damn it, Nick, I'm trying not to swear!"

"How's it going?"

"How the bloody—berry blowtorch!—do you think it's going?!"

"Not very well, by the sound of things."

"Well, flock you, Nick. Flock you."

They stand and stare at each other, Nick holding Dasher's disembodied head under his arm.

"No swearing?" says Nick. "Why? It doesn't suit you."

"Why do you think? Because it's Christmas Eve!"

"Talking about Christmas Eve," says Nick. "We have a problem."

"I know we have a bollocking problem! Why do you think I called you here? Is 'bollocking' a swear word?"

"Yes, I think so."

"I got a call from a very f-f-f fancy lawyer a moment ago."

"Let me guess—"

"Don't bother! You attacked a little girl who tried to climb on your sleigh!"

"That's not what happened."

"They're suing us for damages."

"Damages!" spits Nick. "Ha! They're the ones who—"

"It doesn't matter, Nick!"

"Of course it matters!"

"I can just hear that smart-arsed lawyer in court."

"I think that 'arse' is a swear word."

"He'll be interviewing a child psychologist. Someone already on their payroll. And she'll be going on and on about how this little girl will be scared of Christmas for the rest of her life! Scared of Christmas! Can you imagine?"

"Well, if you had seen what happened..."

"I did! I did see what happened! On the security cameras!"

"Then you'll know that we didn't do anything wrong."

"Nick," says Mr Lowe, rubbing his forehead. "What can I say? It's a bad angle."

Nicholas frowns at his boss. "What do you mean, *a bad angle?*"

"It looks like you *did* attack her."

"You can't be serious."

"It's not pretty, Nick. It's not pretty at all."

"But that ... doesn't make sense. I have a witness!"

"So do they."

"What? Who?"

"It's not important."

"Of course it's bloody important!"

"Berry! Blazing! Bok choy!"

"You sound like you have a unique form of Tourettes."

"I probably do."

Nick drums his fingers on Lowe's desk, then stops and raises a finger. "I've just figured out who this 'witness' is ... and I'm going to kill him!"

"Now, now. This is what I wanted to *avoid*."

"So it *is* him? The little shit!"

"Sugarplum!"

Nick punches the desk. "Argh!"

"He said he'll testify against you."

"Of course he'll testify against me! The imp!"

"We aren't allowed to call him that."

"Well, he *is* an imp."

"Bushy is ... vertically challenged."

"That elf's been after my job since day one!"

"Yes, well, he's about to get it. As from today, you're on proba-tion. This is your final warning, Nick."

"You have *got* to be kidding."

"No more flock-ups, Nick. You hear me? One more ... incident ... and you're out of here. And Bushy will get your job!"

"You can't make Bushy Santa! He's an *elf*!"

"A very ambitious elf. He'll make a good Father Christmas."

"He's three foot four!"

"It won't matter ... when he's sitting up on that sleigh."

"I don't believe you."

"What choice do I have? That family has the power to ruin us!"

"Excuse me. I need to get back. I have work to do."

"No," says Mr Lowe.

"What?"

"I want you to go home."

"What? It's Christmas Eve!"

"Have you looked in the mirror?"

"What's that supposed to mean?"

"Your face is dirty. Your beard is hanging on for dear life. You're carrying around a decapitated reindeer's head, for Holly's sake."

"It's Dasher!"

"Go home, Nick. Clean yourself up. Your job is on the line. Act like it. And—"

"Don't say what I think you're going to say."

"I have to."

"Please, Boss."

"You know the contract clause, Nick. Probation means no seat at the annual Glitter Christmas Feast tomorrow. And no Christmas bonus."

"No! You can't do that! I'm counting on that money!"

"I'm sorry, I don't have a choice."

Nick buries his face in his hands.

"Look," says Mr Lowe. "It's not forever. Once this incident is cleared up, you'll get it. Your cash is already in your envelope. In my drawer! It's just a matter of following the correct procedure."

"You don't understand. I really need that money."

"Don't look at me like that, Nick. You're breaking my heart. Don't take it personally."

"Don't take it personally?"

"It's just protocol."

"You're taking a Christmas bonus away from Father Christmas."

"When you put it that way ... it does seem cruel."

"Is there another way to put it?"

"Damn that clause, hey?" he says, laughing at his own joke. "Get it? Santa Claus?"

"Not funny, boss."

Lowe slaps Nick on the back. "Go home, clean up. I'll see you on your best behaviour tomorrow."

Nicholas can't get the cheesy Christmas carols out of his head as he walks home in the dark. A mangy dog runs up to him and snuffles his hand.

"Not you again!" he says to the stray. "Shoo! Shoo!"

The mutt gets excited and barks. *Is this the beginning of a game?*

Nick carries on walking, and the dog follows him. He turns around and raises his voice. "For the last time, Dog, get lost!"

The stray wags his tail and barks. He's not going anywhere.

"How long have you been waiting?"

He barks again.

Nicholas starts to walk, and the hound trots happily at his side.

"Why don't you follow *that* person home," he says, pointing to a friendly-looking shopper. "Or *that* person? They look like nice people. They'll probably appreciate your unwavering loyalty. Not me. I've got nothing to offer you. I've got nothing to offer anyone. Shoo!"

The dog is still wagging his tail when they reach Nick's block of flats.

Nick sighs. "Look. You're a nice dog, but you can't come in."

The dog angles his head at Nick and whines.

"Don't look at me like that. It's not me, it's you. There are no pets allowed in this building."

He pulls out his keys and opens the main door, sliding his body in sideways, trying to keep the dog out.

"Stay! Stay out there!"

The skinny stray has no problem squeezing through, past Nick's legs.

"No! Naughty dog."

Nick side-eyes the dog as they traipse down the corridor.

"You may have squeezed past me to get into the building but you are *not* coming into my flat."

He unlocks his door. "Best you scram. Go back to the streets."

The stray dog blinks at Nick, and begins to whine.

"Hey, shush," he says. "Be quiet, or you'll have old Mrs Gramercy on your flea-bitten back."

He leaves the dog outside in the corridor, throws his keys on a table and slumps down into his favourite old lazy boy chair. He sighs and closes his eyes, but then the dog whines and scratches the door.

"Dog?" he calls. "Dog! Cut it out!"

A door opens in the corridor and Nick groans. He hears faltering footsteps outside his door, then urgent knocking.

"Nicholas?" calls Mrs Gramercy. "Nicholas?"

"Ugh."

She has some strength in those old arms, evidenced by the enthusiasm of her bashing. This isn't news to Nick: Mrs Gramercy has always made a habit of banging on their shared wall with her walking stick.

"Nicholas! I know you're in there. I'd like a word!"

Nick heaves himself out of his chair and opens the door, and she almost falls through the doorway. He rests his tired head on the cool metal doorframe. "Good evening, Mrs Gramercy. Happy Christmas Eve."

She's a spectre of baby powder and purple rinse. A thin floral jacket is tied around her waist.

"Nicholas *what* is this canine doing here? You *know* that there is a strict *No Pets policy* in this building."

"I do know that."

"Then please explain why this—raggedy animal—is outside your door?"

"I don't know. He followed me home from work. He follows me home every day. Today he slipped through the front door—I couldn't stop him."

"This is unacceptable!"

Nick rubs his eyes. "I'm sorry, Mrs Gramercy. I'm not sure what to do about it."

"Well, you should take him outside at the very least! Where he belongs! Or to the SPCA!"

"Okay, Mrs Gramercy," he starts to close the door. "Have a nice evening, then."

The old woman jams her Green Cross in the way. "And another thing!"

"I know, I know. My music is too loud."

She shakes a bony finger at him, and the dog whines. "Your music is too loud!"

"But I'm not playing any music."

"It's *too loud*, Nicholas!"

"I'll turn it down, Mrs Gramercy."

She crimps her lips at the dog and walks back to her flat, slamming the door.

"Happy Christmas Eve!" he shouts.

The dog looks up at him and pants.

"Well, then, Dog. You'd better come in."

Hinges squeak as Nick opens the kitchen cupboards. "There's no food in the house. I'm only getting paid tomorrow. Hopefully. You want some water?"

He puts down a cereal bowl of water at the foot of the couch, and slumps back into his chair.

"Finally," he says, and sighs. "Some peace and quiet. It's all I wanted." The dog watches him. "I spend the whole day asking people what *they want* for Christmas. Do you think anyone ever bothers to ask what *I want*?"

There is a bustling sound outside the window, on the street. The dog's ears prick up, and he barks.

"Shhh," says Nick.

The group of people begin to sing *Jingle Bells*.

"You have *got* to be kidding me."

Nick hauls himself out of his chair again and stomps to the window. He pushes his head through the frame and shouts down at the choir.

"Get lost! Just get lost! *Hey! Get out of here!*"

The choir stops mid-song and moves along quickly. Nick slams the window shut.

The next morning, Nick is late for work, and in his rush he walks straight into Mr Rens as he's leaving the building.

"Nick!" says his landlord.

"Mr Rens! Merry Christmas!"

"What is 'merry' about it?"

The dog looks up at Mr Rens and barks his happy bark.

"Look," says Nick, scratching his head. "About the dog. I can explain."

"I don't give a fig about the dog."

"Really?"

"Sometimes—no, ALL the time—I prefer dogs to people."

"Well," says Nick. "I think I know what you mean."

"The problem is, as you know … that rent … is late. Very late."

"I know! I meant to speak to you about it. I'm getting it. I'm getting the money today."

"*Today*, Nicholas, or that flat will be padlocked and there'll be a big fat eviction notice on the door. Got it?"

Mr Rens pats the dog and walks away.

Nicholas calls after him. "You'd evict someone on Christmas Day?"

His landlord stops and turns back to face him. "I think you know the answer to that."

❖

"Thanks, Brenda, I really appreciate you helping me with this," says Nick.

Brenda beams at him. "Of course! Poor Dasher, we have to fix him, don't we?"

"Don't want the kids being scared off by a headless reindeer."

"It's better to be scared off by a grumpy Father Christmas?"

"Grumpy?" says Nick. "This is my happy face."

"Ha."

"It's not the first time the sleigh has been damaged. It was my father's before it was mine."

"How old is it? It looks ancient."

"It's an antique! Besides, I'm sure that anything not made out of plastic seems ancient to your generation."

"You're not *that* much older than me, you know?"

"Er ... yes, I am," he says.

They pack up the tools and sweep up the sawdust.

"Okay, well, it looks pretty good," says Brenda. "As good as new?"

Nick slaps Dasher's neck affectionately. "Hardly, but it will do."

"Look at that, it's time for the big show! I need to announce it. See you later? At the annual Christmas Feast?"

"Maybe."

"Maybe? But you can't miss the Feast! It's the best part of Glitter Christmas! You're head of the table! What will a Christmas Feast be without Father Christmas?"

"Not sure if I'm invited after what happened yesterday."

"Argh!" She claws the air in between them like an angry bear.

"Go!" says Nick, pushing her off. "You're late."

"Hey Santa!" says Ferdi, ambling up to the repaired sleigh. "I see the chariot is ready for the onslaught."

Brenda's voice comes over the sound system.

Ding-aling-aling!

"Merry Christmas shoppers! We hope you are having a merry shopping experience here at Glitter Mall. Remember that Pretty Pictures..."

Ferdi leans in. "You know what I don't get? Who wants to be in a shopping mall on Christmas Day?"

" ...Make your home as pretty as a picture!..."

Ferdi polishes his camera, and blows on it to dislodge a speck of dust on the lens. "I mean, I know *we're* here, but it's not like we have a choice."

"...Cheeses of Nazareth is having a special on all things cheesy. And now for the big news! Father Christmas and his elves are at the North Pole and they're waiting for you! It's time for the annual *Climb on the Sleigh with Father Christmas!* (The North Pole is on the first floor in the square in front of Homemakers Inc.). See you there! Ho ho ho!"

The Christmas carols fade back in, louder than before.

"And... off we go," says Ferdi, holding up his camera. "It's your moment of glory. May the merry mayhem commence!"

Nick hauls himself up onto his sleigh and there is a stampede of excited children.

"I wanna go up there with Santa!"

"Hello Father Kissmas! Hello Father Kissmas!"

"I'm on the sleigh!"

"Hello Rudolph! Hello Rudolph!"

"Look at me, Mommy! I'm on the sleigh!"

"Up! Up! Mama! Up!"

"I'm gonna drive the sleigh! Watch me, Mommy, I'm driving the sleigh!"

Nick recognises the boy from yesterday—David—and his baby sister. He's wearing a red T-Rex shirt today, and pretending to steer the sleigh.

"Ah, hello again. That's very good driving, young man."

His baby sister is on her mother's hip: a kind-looking woman in a blue dress. When she sees Nick, she swoons. "Hello Father Kissmas!"

Ferdi is snapping like a madman, and Nick blinks away the bright white flashes in his eyes.

The boy pats him on his knee. "Do you think that I could be a Father Christmas one day?"

"Hmmm..." says Nick. "I don't know..."

Another child near them gives an excited sob.

"Only ve-e-ery special boys are allowed to become Father Christmas."

David's face falls.

"But you know what?" says Nick. "I think you've got what it takes!"

"Hello Ma'am," says Ferdi to the fawning mother. He points at

David and Nick. "Let me take a picture of your lovely little boy. It's only R49.99 and it's a memory you can treasure forever!"

"Oh, yes please," she gushes, hugging her baby closer. "How special!"

Suddenly there is a noise in the ceiling. A clunking. They all look up.

"What is that strange sound?"

"It's the snow!" says Ferdi. "The snow machine! It's coming ... wait for it..."

The sound gets louder and then the ceiling explodes with fake snow that flutters down on everyone. The kids go crazy.

"It's like it's really snowing!" says the mother. "Look at the kids! They're loving it!"

The photographer is shooting every child at every angle.

"Wait," says the woman, sniffing. "What's that smell?"

"Hey?"

"That smell ... like something's ... burning ..."

A parent on the other side of the sleigh starts screaming. "Fire! Fire!"

All hell breaks loose as everyone panics. Parents shriek and scramble for their children, and the kids all start crying. Nicholas offloads the children as fast as he can. The fire alarm blares.

"Get off the sleigh!" screams the woman in blue. "It's burning! It's on fire! David!"

Ferdi takes the baby girl from her to free up her hands. The baby looks worried and says "Hot!"

The sleigh bursts into bright orange flames. There is more screaming and clambering. Shrieking and coughing.

"My son!" shouts the woman. "I can't see him! Help! Help!"

Ferdi stops the woman from running into the flames. "No! Don't go in there!"

"Let me go!" she yells. "I have to get my boy!

"Look!" he says. "Father Christmas has him! He's safe."

Nicholas drops David down onto the floor and he runs towards his mom.

"David!" They hug and the woman sobs into his T-Rex chest.

"Father Christmas saved me!" he says. "Father Christmas saved everyone!"

"Not everyone," says Ferdi, pointing. "Look, Bushy Evergreen is still on the sleigh!"

"The elf!" says David. "The elf is burning!"

Bushy's synthetic costume is highly flammable; he hops as flames leap up his legs and back.

The baby shouts "Elf! Hot!"

Ferdi shouts at Nick. "Don't go back, Nick, you're crazy! You'll be incinerated! Don't do it!"

But Nicholas launches himself into the fire to save Bushy. There is another explosion, and then the sound of a fire truck approaching.

❖

"Flapping firehoses, Nick," says Mr Lowe. "You had us so worried!"

Brenda holds his hand. "Are you *sure* you're okay?"

"It's not anything a shower won't sort out," says Nick. "And a haircut."

"Well, you are an absolute *hero*," says Brenda. "You must have saved twenty children today!"

"And an elf!" says Lowe.

Brenda laughs. "Twenty children and an elf!"

Mr Lowe's face darkens. "An elf who didn't deserve to be saved!"

"What?" asks Nick. "What do you mean, didn't deserve to be saved?"

"It's all on camera, Nick," says Lowe. "The whole F-F-fiery disaster. And it was started by no one other than a naughty elf who knocked over a Christmas tree candle. On purpose!"

"I told you he was an imp!"

"Yes, well, he's no longer in the employ of Glitter Mall, that's for sure! But you, Nick, you're guaranteed of a job for as long as you want it."

"I don't have a sleigh anymore."

"We'll buy you a new one!" says Lowe. "A brand new one, with all the bells and whistles."

"My Santa uniform is ruined."

"We had to cut it off you. What was left of it."

"None of that matters," says Lowe.

"But you see," says Nick. "It does."

"If you're worried about that little brat who kicked you in the shins—" says Lowe.

"They've dropped the lawsuit," says Brenda. "Ferdi got the whole thing on his camera. It shows clearly that you did nothing wrong."

"Which means," says Lowe. "That your place at the head of the Annual Christmas Feast is waiting for you."

"We're still having the feast? After all of this?"

"Of course we are!" Lowe slaps Nick on the back. "It's an annual tradition! We have three roast chickens and a ham waiting for us! And Christmas pudding! Although I think we'll skip lighting the brandy this year..."

"Listen, Boss," says Nick. "I'm resigning. You see that singed Santa hat on the floor?"

"Yes?"

"Take that as my formal resignation.

"Is it about your bonus? Of course you can have it now, you deserve every cent!"

Lowe takes an envelope out of his drawer and hands it to Nick, who tucks it into his pocket.

"Thank you. But I'm still resigning."

"You can't resign! You've been Glitter Mall's Father Christmas since ... since the beginning of time!"

Brenda's eyes are shining with tears. "It won't be the same without you!"

"Bren," says Nick.

She sniffs and looks at him. "Yes?"

"Can I have that chicken in a take-away container?"

She looks horrified. "No!"

"No?"

"I just mean ... please don't. Stay and eat with us!"

"I can't," says Nick. "I have to be somewhere."

Nicholas looks up at the faded façade of the Glitter Mall as he leaves. It's dark but the stars are out, and the moon. He breathes in the night sky.

"Goodbye, Glitter Mall."

The dog barks.

"Ah," says Nick. "Hello Dog."

He gives it a scratch behind the ears, and the dog wags his tail.

"Come on, let's go."

Nicholas unlocks the door to his building. This time, the dog waits to be invited.

"Well? What are you waiting for?" says Nick, and the mutt rushes in.

"Good boy."

They walk to the landlord's flat together and knock on the door.

"And?" demands Mr Rens. "What happened to you?"

"There was an ... accident ... at work."

"An accident?" He laughs. "It looks like you were dragged through a chimney backwards."

"Ja, well," says Nick.

"You still have the hound."

The skinny dog barks.

"Yip. I've named him Dasher."

"Dasher? That's a good name."

Rens pats the dog, scrubs him behind the ears.

"I have the money," says Nick, handing over the envelope from his pocket. "For Mrs Gramercy's rent."

Rens takes it, shaking his head. "I don't get it."

"What?"

"I don't get why you're paying her rent. She's a grumpy old bag.

Always giving you trouble. I would think you'd *want* her evicted. Why are you doing this?"

Dasher barks and jumps up.

Nicholas shrugs. "Because it's Christmas."

When they get to Nick's flat he tops up Dasher's water bowl and fetches another. He scoops the roast chicken into it and puts it on the floor; pats the dog's head, runs his hand over his jutting ribs.

When Dasher finishes his dinner he jumps up onto Nick's lap, and Nick strokes him. He relaxes back into his favourite chair with a loud sigh.

"Finally," he says, as he closes his eyes. "Finally. Some peace and quiet."

There is a loud banging on the wall in the kitchen. It's Mrs Gramercy with her walking stick.

"Turn down that blasted music!" she shouts.

Nick laughs. He feels free; no longer weighted down by the family sleigh.

He shouts back at the wall. "Merry Christmas, Mrs Gramercy!"

~

11

KAKKERLAK

THEY SAY the only good cockroach is a dead cockroach. And even then the encounter is not usually described as a pleasant one. The word itself whiffs of trash and rot, death and decay. The name in my mother tongue, Afrikaans, is far more poetic: you can't help saying it out loud: *Kakkerlak*. The tongue dances on the roof of your mouth and, bowing, finishes on the gratifying sharp 'k'.

There is a hailstorm of bullets outside. Sharp steel stones that rip through plaster and glass in untidy explosions. I'm surprised there are still bullets left in this world.

There is a scream. Human. It's a faraway sound, far enough away for it not to drill into my head. It's muffled by meters of time and space and wastebodiesbonesburning. Sweet meat smoke. At least they can scream. They are alive. Heat streams at me, burning my six brittle legs, forcing me to scurry, reminding me that I, too, am living, whether I want to be or not.

There are bullets but there is no food. The Führer would have been pleased (I can't remember what butter tastes like). Against all odds I found a postage stamp and have been eating its glue. I'm under a brick, that's under a beam, that's under a rooftile, that used to be a house: A building which used to be someone's home. I try to imagine what it was like. A neat rectangle of rooms with carpets and curtains. A bedroom, a bathroom, a kitchen, a kitchen drawer that rolls open without sticking.

It's a pretty stamp, full of petals. Namaqualand Daisies, maybe, I'm not sure. Flowers only live in dreams, now; there is colour only in imagination. God knows how this square miracle of a blooming postage stamp survived this civil war.

Perhaps there are still flowers in other parts of the world. We have no way of knowing if this apocalypse is exclusively inherent to South Africa. No radio or TV or news. Maybe the rest of the world has also exploded. Or maybe they are living in a clean bubble of declination: at last relinquishing Africa to the Africans. When they closed their borders to us in '86 we were sure it was a temporary measure. Berlinesque: A wall, ready to fall. Besides, only people rich enough to buy plane tickets would be able to take refuge in Europe, Australia, America. They should have welcomed the wealthy expats: Doctors, lawyers, engineers. It's not like they had to deal with ragged lice-infested fugitives camping at their borders, scratching for hand-outs like our neighbouring countries had to. The West's walls went up, regardless. The walls went up and they never came down.

Pre-wall: We decided to stay, despite my wife begging me to

leave. It wasn't because I had hope. It was because I was caught by my duty to my country: A rusty rat trap; flypaper. I thought that if we fought hard enough we could stop South Africa's descent into hell. Thought we could, in some way, hold onto that which was ours. We were the 90s version of the *Bittereinders*. A hundred-year-old lesson we failed to learn.

When the crocodile liberators known as the Freedom Fighters overthrew the government they renamed the country *Inkululeko*—Freedom—but no one took much notice. When your house has been burned to nothing and your family sleep forever in a shallow grave, you stop caring about abstractions like place names. Our duty was to stop the FF at all costs. Before that we were called the Special Branch and our job was to monitor any treasonous movements caught resisting or plotting against Apartheid. After a while intelligence was not enough, and we had to take certain matters into our own hands. Bantu was one of those matters. Before him: Kgoathe; Modipane. Other nameless faces that still come to me, involuntarily fluttering my wings. But Bantu's death was a victory. We celebrated that day with our families: sun-warmed tins of Lion lager, potato salad and *braaivleis* in our vast back gardens. Peppermint Crisp tart. Coffee and *Herzoggies*. Shiny pink foreheads, bulging khaki bellies. Colours leak in and stain my memories.

An eruption rocks the earth. It's difficult to tell who is fighting whom nowadays. It used to be simple: The majority fighting the minority for their liberty. The minority with their claws so deeply hooked in the upside-down-inside-out reality they had created for themselves: the idea that this country belonged to them ... that this country belonged to *us*. I was one of them, after all.

In a world of colour it was Black versus White. Politicians and terrorists and cops spilling blood of equal redness in equal measure until you could no longer distinguish who the terrorists were (turns out we were all terrorists). When President Botha was assassinated we didn't leave our house for a week. Double-bolted the doors and lived off our emergency supplies of Koo beans, canned *koejawels* and a bulk pack of Bar-Ones. Then Viljoen came in, took over, and we came up for air.

One of the terrorists we had imprisoned on Robben Island—one of the biggest troublemakers—had managed to drum up support overseas, and there was pressure to release him, despite the innocent lives he had claimed. He was a popular leader and there was talk, locally, of him becoming the next president of South Africa. We laughed into our brandy and Cokes.

Viljoen organised a press junket to show the world on a live broadcast that one of their struggle heroes was to be a free man. People lined the streets for kilometres with their placards and bright yellow shirts. During his speech his skull was ripped apart by a lead soft-point, boat-tailed, copper-jacketed bullet. He fell backwards into his family's arms. Everyone went *bedol,* and that was the end of South Africa. *Inkululeko.*

Of course it had always been inevitable. The arrogant Few can only hold down the ardent Many for so long before there is thunder. No one knew who held the sighted rifle that day but everyone suspected the Afrikaner Reactionaries. A quasi-religious violent splinter group from the AWB, the AR would detonate seven bombs for each one planted by *Umkhonto We Sizwe*. The Reactionaries were a volatile group: a dangerous combination of lack of expertise and excess of emotion. Big bombs, short fuses. They would often end up killing their own—our own. They believed the government was in the process of giving their country away, and would do anything to prevent that from happening. Before the assassination we monitored them as closely as the Freedom Fighters, but we were, of course, more sympathetic to their cause. They were our own delinquent teenage sons.

I had a son, once. A son and two daughters, all blond-haired. But there is no use in thinking about that now.

A state of emergency was declared. We had tanks and Kaspirs in the streets—not only in the townships but also in our scrubbed white suburbs. School kids were gunned down in golden sunshine; green farms scorched black. Nights of the Long Knives bled incarnadine: a continent of *meids* and *garden-boys* stalked and snatched their employers' lives while they slept. Mothers took their own lives, and the sky that used to be so vital and blue was damned to monochrome. Fevered children resisted sleep with their eyes wide, and rolling in terror. I remember holding their clammy little hands; pale skin always sweet-smelling. Their fear scratched at my soul. Sleepless nights of counting our gifts: The children were scared, but they were breathing.

Sometimes, when I can no longer think of what is real, I

abandon it for fantasies of what my life may have been like. What my daughters would look like, what my son would be doing for a living, the feel of my wife's warm skin against my chest. Anniversaries, birthdays, weddings. Dare I imagine balloons, or a cake? So wonderful and other-worldly. I dream of having a human body again. I dream of a hot shower, even though I know that there is neither electricity nor water. The mad luxury of showering with drinking water! It seems impossible now. Surely it never existed. One of the crazy creations of my mind, like the green crispness of an apple or the feeling of a clean cotton pillow on my cheek. Now I keep company with mangy rats and maggots.

I am condemned to the darkness. Cockroaches, being nocturnal, flee from light. Soft tongue against palate: *kakkerlak.*

Inkululeko.

In a way I chose this condemnation. I knew what we were doing was against god, even in that godless reality. The thin pages of bibles made good fire-starters. Most saved them till the other books were burnt. I had no such scruples.

I gave up praying a long time ago. A prayer has never brought anyone back, never squeezed a heart to live, never pumped lost blood back into a child's washed-out body. My own heart is ancient and thick with scars. Its grizzled complaint: What do I want with a god who allows such atrocities to happen? We were so certain of him before: singing and sweating in claustrophobic churches; studying that Black Book; shaking, kneeling, gnashing, speaking in tongues.

The power we felt! The blessings we had. He was everything, He would provide, we were His Chosen Ones. I don't know who forsook who first, but soon it became clear that he was no longer interested in our variety of lamb. It's not like he chose the other side, either, the black sheep. They prayed just as hard as we did, but they were just as condemned, and just as abandoned. Now, godless, I still sweat, and shake, and kneel, and gnash. The only difference is that now I know it's all meaningless. Now Christ is nothing but a curse-word.

The day I chose this destiny was an ordinary day. Scrambled eggs on toast, fresh orange juice, too tart for my taste. We always ate breakfast together because I worked late and didn't always make it home in time for dinner (everyday feasts of Breakfast, Lunch, Dinner: these concepts are now extinct). Cornflakes, caramel-coloured toast and fresh white milk for the children. Could that be true?

We had a man in custody—Ngubane—we had detained him two weeks prior and he was beginning to overstay his welcome. Despite sincere beatings he refused us any information and we were growing tired of his hard-headedness. It's not that he didn't feel the pain: his screams helped loosen the tongues of many of his neighbours. His stubbornness enraged us. That day, his face was still swollen from the week before, when a colleague gave him a *seep-in-'n-sok klap*: a beating with a bar of soap in a sock. The guard had reported that Ngubane slept sitting up, evidence of broken ribs. Even if he chose to speak that day we wouldn't have been able to release him (rubbery lips split scabby). There would be too many questions about our interview methods. What the press and pinkos and liberal whiteys didn't understand was that we were doing it for them as much as for our own families. The fear of the Blacks—the Others—governing our country eclipsed the fear of any other outcome. What if they decided to take revenge?

I wanted to give Ngubane a chance. I didn't enjoy torturing detainees. It made me feel *naar,* despite my experience in the field. I tried to be civil, even friendly, to soften him up. I purred into his ear. Didn't he understand that we needed the intelligence he had to make the country a safe place to live? That we have his people's best interests at heart? The smell of stale urine was like smoke in our nostrils. Fleas jumped. Did he know that if he talked to me, told me what I needed to know, that he may have saved a life, possibly many? Sour body odour in my movements, and in his stillness. It could mean one less bullet in the back of a child, I remember saying. His dark skin was oily, and it repulsed me. I told him of how his wife had come to bring him fresh clothes and how he could go home to her if he simply co-operated. *She's staying with your sister in Pimville, Ngubane, now isn't that good to know?*

Only a slight change in his breathing gave his emotion away. His wet copper eyes continued their defiant appraisal of the cell wall. *Maybe we should pay your wife a visit tonight,* I suggested. I walked my fingers along the bars of the cell, crinkled my eyes. I mentioned that I would take a few men along with me to make sure that she was thoroughly... interrogated. He tried to ignore the electric undercurrent of my threat but his breathing betrayed him. Double-crossed by his own heart and lungs.

His body—motionless—an ant in amber. Ngubane was a master at hiding his pain. Hot breath, but not a word spilt. My temper chewed at my nerves. The fuse was lit.

This insolent Black!

Something inside me seized up and fractured, sending shards of violence into every fibre of my body. I wanted to smash his swollen head against the cement floor. Instead I called for the plastic bag.

I had killed men before but never in such a pre-meditated way, and never out of rage. He struggled against me, and I kept squeezing. It was my defining moment, my becoming.

What is the opposite of redemption?

I felt something leave my body as his unfaithful heart stopped beating, as if I was the one dying.

As if I was the one dying.

When his tremor subsided, I loosened my grip on the blue bag, and some ascending ghost pulled on my intestines as if it didn't want to go. That day I changed. That second. From then on the mirror showed me empty sockets instead of eyes, and sleep was slippery.

When I lost the girls I lost part of my mind. Ivory skin slashed with crimson ribbons. Rubies half-hidden in flesh-alabaster. Their fingers were cold by the time I touched them.

After finding the girls with their opened throats I knew that my wife and son were lost to me, too. It was just a matter of time. I was too numb to feel the detonation that took their lives and one of my arms. Numb. Deafanddumb. It wasn't a kindred curse: the same tragedy was playing out with neighbours and colleagues and far-flung friends. It seemed to me then that no one was to survive the sudden civil war.

My own death was expected. After a year of surviving my family, I was pinned between living and having no life. A weighted, weightless limbo. By then I was fighting under the more nebulous White Arm that included all the surviving whites in the country. Female and child soldiers were allocated the more precise weapons: guns and hand grenades. We had knives, metal poles, fists, knees, and teeth. Our values were necklaced: morality was trussed up with rubber tyres, doused with petrol, and set alight. Giant toppling acrid piles spitting fire.

We reminded ourselves every day that we had been right to fear the Blacks. We knew that if the Blacks ever took over the country it would be raped and ruined. Our nightmare had been realised. We had been right to keep them under control for as long as we could.

My postage stamp glue is nearly finished. I wonder how long I will survive without food. I guess at three months. And then what? There are thousands of us. Will cockroach cannibalise cockroach? Will the cockroach inherit the earth? I am tired of this life. Exhausted by every barbed minute. Part of my punishment is to have no way out. I have crawled into stinking toxic puddles and crackling fires but still I live. Cursed to outlive my breaking point again and again until ... what? What comes after reincarnation, if that is what this curse is? Bantu, Kgoathe, Modipane, Ngubane ... Louise, Neil, Nora, Analette ... I wonder where they are.

It wasn't only god who turned away from us, nature did too. Buds stopped blooming and fruiting, and vegetables turned to poisoned stones. She came at us with everything in her arsenal: brown floods, biting insects, diseases that stole throats and eyes from everyone it touched, with a particular reach and fondness for babies. Soon babies stopped being born at all. Some famines are crueller than lack of food.

Towards my human end we all had shaved heads and wore rags for hats. Sometimes it was hard to tell if someone was white or black because of the dirt and grease we used as camouflage. Our killing was mostly intuitive: we were a cackle of hyenas. But sometimes in the chaos of hail and smoke we would get it wrong. We shot one of our women in the stomach. We blew up a fellow fighter. We had been right. We had been right.

Ngubane's swollen unspeaking lips used to taunt me, haunt me, on those restless nights. I see his dusty-eyed wife, hopeful with her fresh laundry; I hear his snapping ribs, feel his red breath spattered on my neck.

I was ransacking a house, looking for food—looking for anything —and found death hidden in a kitchen drawer. A dark game of potluck. It was a surprise, but I was ready for it. I didn't know I had died until I woke up in this hard shell. A booby trap: a Special Branch trick. How the gods must have laughed.

A bright white explosion followed by... the friable ether of nothingness.

An urge to breathe deep the pale air. A vacuum in my head: A lightness. The world had opened itself up to me, showing its core of warm white, and an unutterable sense of relief.

I was free for a moment. A sweet second. A sob. My body stretched from the ground to the clouds in a backward dive. Sweet oblivion—an ant in honey?—then something holds me, catches me, pulls me to the ground. The sky closes. My bleached family lie crumpled at my feet, lost in my dark shadow. The shadow that is Bantu, Kgoathe, Modipane, Ngubane. The darkness I can't escape now as I sit hissing in this hole. Hissing. Scuttling. Dreaming of death's head.

Things were simpler then: Black and White. A burnt-out-coconut republic. It was such a long time ago. Now there is no colour barrier. A man kills another man for his food no matter the pigment of his skin. Gangs of marauders patrol the streets looking for women to rape and body parts to roast over open flame. Who cares if a monster is black or white? We were right, we were right. We were so very wrong.

There are no children. Soon there will only be cockroaches. *Kakkerlakke. Inkululeko.*

The world is painted grey. We got our justice. They got their equality. We are them and they are us. The country is truly colour-blind.

~

12

THE BRAIN BLEACHER

Do you know that most moments don't leave a trace?

Think about it. It's disturbing.

Only the most striking parts of your existence are remembered, which means that you don't remember the majority of your life. You have, roughly, the three seconds of your present moment, plus a (mostly inaccurate, and decaying) memory of around one percent of your past, and that's it. The rest fades away.

Who are you?

What have you done?

Does any of it matter?

The doorbell rings, and I take my time in answering it. Outside, in the smoky orange autumn air, stand a couple with matching frowns. Marriage counselling is usually below my pay grade—I'm a neuroscientist—but Mrs King had begged me over the phone. She was sick with guilt and regret; her husband was no longer talking to her. I was busy and non-committal at the time and suggested they see a relationship therapist, but she was adamant. She'd pay double my regular fees, she said, triple, so I agreed to take their case. (I'll charge her half; it's not like I need the money).

I lead the Kings into my neat lounge, which doubles as my consulting room, and settle them with tea. It's professional enough—I've recently downsized and embraced super-mini-malism—so it's not unlike a psychiatrist's room, if you ignore the blinking lights and the hum of my electronic equipment.

Mr King eyes my whisky cabinet, but booze and brain manipu-lation is seldom a good idea. The troubled couple sit up straight, not touching, not looking at one another.

"I had an affair," says Mrs King, and Mr King winces. A kick in the shins.

"I see."

I watch them without judgement, but also without warmth. It's best to not get emotionally involved in these things.

She squirms. "I feel terrible about it. I'll always feel terrible."

I turn to Mr King. "And how do you feel?"

His cheeks colour, his balding head shines. His mouth is crimped downwards.

"He's angry," she says. "Bitter. He'll never forgive me as long as he lives."

I look at Mr King, still waiting for an answer, but none is forthcoming.

"It wasn't really an *affair*," she says. "Just a once-off thing, a stupid thing. I had had too much to drink at an office party. It didn't mean anything."

"You always say that," says Mr King in a low voice that simmers with fury.

"What?"

"You always say it didn't mean anything, as if that somehow mitigates the betrayal."

"You know what I mean." Her eyes are moist, and pleading.

"So you risked our entire marriage for someone *who didn't mean anything to you*," says Mr King. "And you think that will make me feel better."

"I don't mean it like that," she says. "I just mean I don't have feelings for him."

"It doesn't matter," he says, turning his head further away, and looking at the blank wall. "It doesn't matter anymore."

Mrs King shoots me another look of desperation.

"He wants a divorce. Sixteen years of a bloody good marriage and he wants to throw it all away."

"I'm not the one," he murmurs, "who threw it all away."

"He'll never forgive me. He lords it over me every day. Won't touch me, or talk to me."

Mrs King crosses her arms and falls back into the couch. I think she's about to sulk but then I see silent tears rushing down her face. The Kings haven't touched their tea.

"Okay," I say. This seems like a pretty straightforward case."You'd like your husband's knowledge of the affair erased?"

They nod, and Mrs King speaks again. "And mine. I want to feel as if it never happened."

Personally, I don't think it will work. I mean, I can erase the affair, but I can't erase the underlying reason for the affair. People in happy marriages seldom cheat.

I place my hands on my knees and smile. "That seems like a good solution."

I don't think it will save their relationship, but I'll try my best to delete all the pain I can.

Mrs King sits up again, and wipes the mascara from under her eyes. "Does that mean you'll do it for us?"

"We can do it this afternoon, if you like," I say. "Right now. It's a relatively simple process."

Mrs King's face crumples up again. "Thank you," she sobs. "Thank you."

I of all people know that no one is immune to blunders.

Before we begin, I have one more question for them.

"If you were to go on a second honeymoon, where would you go?"

I take them to separate, but connected, rooms and ready my equipment. I place one of the helmets on Mrs King's head, and I back up her prefrontal cortex, and get to work erasing the dalliance which has caused so much trouble (tequila and pineapple shooters; cheap white wine in a paper cup; 80s music; two minutes against the hard edge of an office desk;

vomiting into a garden bed painted black by the night sky). If I didn't care about Mrs King I would limit my work to that, but instead I track through the subsequent memories: the confession, the fights, the stonewalling, and I plant a false memory there, instead. A second honeymoon in Franschhoek where the couple eat at expensive restaurants, go for long walks and wine-tasting, and have particularly good sex.

Once you've had a memory erased, it's common to feel that something is missing. It was a thought-loop that was taking up a lot of your mental bandwidth, and now it's gone. The brain abhors a vacuum, and you no longer have that thing to reach for. Yes, you reach for bad memories, even though the experience is unpleasant. It's like the compulsion to probe a sore tooth with a tongue: it's difficult to just leave the pain alone. So I replace the bad memories with happy simulations. It's not challenging; your brain does most of the work. I just plant the seed and give it a loose structure, and your imagination does the rest. For Mr and Mrs King's second honeymoon I process a paired simulation, so that they have equal creative contributions. Perhaps Mrs King wanted to waterski, but Mr King wanted to read. It's no problem when their neural pathways are connected.

You might think it's morally wrong or overly manipulative to plant a false memory. It may remind you of that troubling branch of psychotherapy which was popular in the 90s that resulted in patients mixing up their dream analysis with uncovering supposedly repressed memories, with consequences of false accusations of physical and sexual abuse, alien abduction, and demonic possession. But I have no ethical ambivalence about what I do. If I can make someone happier—whatever that means—with the tools I have, why wouldn't I?

You could say it's like hypnotherapy, but on a much deeper

level: at a cellular level, because it's not only your brain that holds memories.

A client of mine brought her obese son in last week. Zayd's eight years old and weighs close to seventy kilograms. He hates exercise and is addicted to gaming and junk food, and his poor mother was desperate and out of options. This time I planted unpleasant memories: I simulated bouts of food poisoning from candy and fast food, and added feelings of intense anxiety and grief associated with his GamerSlate.

But it wasn't all doom and gloom. I added a few happy moments that revolved around running, swimming and basketball, and did some positive reinforcement of healthy food.

But that's like lying! I hear you say. *Lying to a child!*

Well, the Tooth Fairy would not be happy, would she? Nor would Santa Claus.

You think playing with memory is a dangerous thing and the truth is, it can be. You think planting false memories, no matter the positive outcome, must be a bad idea. What you don't know is that memory is extremely fragile. It's a grey, delicate, wavering thing. You think your memory of an important event is exactly how it happened? You're wrong. Even the most observant people make everyday memory mistakes.

This has been proven over and over again in criminal courts. Eye witnesses who swear they saw something—or didn't see something—are often flat-out wrong. Around three quarters of the convicts exonerated in the US due to DNA technology were behind bars because of incorrect witness testimony.

I often tell my clients to be careful what they remember. Some of them laugh, assuming I'm joking, but the more intuitive ones heed my advice. Not every memory will serve you.

While a memory is a mental snapshot of a moment, it carries with it layers of emotion and texture and scent. Your experience will differ to the person who is standing right next to you, and as the moment is imprinted in your brain, it's coloured by your mood and life experiences.

People mistake their experience for the truth.

Memories are constructed and reconstructed. So if your memory is not as black-and-white as you imagine, if it's open to suggestion (your own and other people's) then manipulating it a little here and there seems less wrong, doesn't it?

A moment of high emotional intensity will always create the most vivid memory. Where were you when the Twin Towers fell? Yes, of course, you remember. Weddings, births, deaths, these are our emotional cornerstones, days we need no help recalling. When it comes to bad memories, the mind naturally tries to suppress them, but this takes a lot of mental energy. It's not a healthy state of mind, not if you, like most of the people on this earth, are eternally reaching for happiness.

That's where I come in.

I'm the eraser, the brain bleacher, the memory hacker. It's an easy, neat job to shine someone's mind. I back up each client's memory three ways before I do any cognitive washing. Some-times there are glitches, errors, corrupted disks, but these things can usually be solved. The problems come in when clients want to remember what they previously paid to forget.

I leave Mrs King to luxuriate in her holiday simulation while I start on Mr King. After a successful back-up I scroll through his recent memory, to scrub out his wife's confession and ensuing arguments, but I stop when I find something interesting.

He's outside a hotel in Cape Town, wearing a smart suit. I can see his reflection in the high-gloss hotel exterior, with cars zooming in the background. Business trip, I think, expecting to see a boardroom meeting, perhaps a lunch overlooking the ocean. Instead he spends hours in his hotel room, watching porn and smoking cigarettes. Eventually she arrives: a five-foot-ten blonde bimbo with a dress that hardly covers her nipples. A prostitute? No, a mistress.

I sigh.

Really, Mr King?

What a shame. What a cliché. It would be forgivable if he wasn't being such an asshole to his wife, allowing her to self-flagellate when his betrayal is so much more ambitious than hers. This affair isn't a once-off mistake. I see the same woman over and over in his memory, going back years. It takes me an hour to get rid of her. This extra work annoys me, and to make myself feel better I add a small accident to their otherwise idyllic second honeymoon. In an unfortunate incident, Mr King is distracted by a poster of a bikini-clad supermodel on the wall of a public restroom and gets his penis stuck in his zipper. I'm happy with the result.

I don't stop there. I pickpocket his phone and erase all communication from his mistress (there isn't much: Mr King is an expert at covering his tracks) and I delete her contact information. I'm almost sorry I won't be a fly on the wall when she tries to call him again.

When we're finished, I lead the Kings to the front door. They both seem a bit disoriented, which isn't unusual. They'll catch an Uber home and have a rest, allowing their minds to consolidate the new memories. I wave them goodbye and wish them happiness, and wonder if they'll ever be back. I'm glad I accepted their case; I found dealing with Mr King's mistress especially satisfying.

I don't take on all the clients that come my way. One of the first jobs I was ambivalent about accepting was to shine the mind of a young woman who couldn't get over the heartache of a miscarriage. Her doctor—a friend of mine from med school—recommended she see me. Over a glass of pinot noir on his balcony overlooking Table Mountain he told me about her case. The woman was young and healthy and in a happy marriage, but she had suffered a traumatic miscarriage (started bleeding while on a crowded train; couldn't get hold of her husband; had to get off and walk in a neighbourhood not familiar to her, bleeding and almost bent double by painful cramps). The overwhelming grief combined with the humiliation and anguish of the event scarred her. She started avoiding sex with her husband, and changed the subject when he tried to discuss trying to conceive again.

I did hesitate to treat her. I wondered what the implications of voiding her grief would be. I felt that erasing her memory of the miscarriage would, in a way, be erasing the baby, too, and that made me feel uncomfortable.

I know from experience that it's important to process these things, to accept your loss in order to move beyond it, but the more I got to know her, the more I realised there was no advantage in her remembering that day. She was sliding into depression and wrecking her relationship on the way down, so I agreed. I haven't seen her since the erasure, but my doctor friend tells me she is on the mend. I didn't ask for details. I do still think of that baby, though. I have dreams that he or she is floating in the cosmos, lost in space.

Another would-be client was devastated by the loss of her Siamese cat and asked me to bleach her memories of him. I explained to her that although she was feeling shattered now, the pain would ease and she'd soon be able to remember him with joy and affection. They had shared sixteen happy years together. It would be a shame to strip that from her life. I turned that job down.

I think that was a good call, but sometimes I make mistakes.

A man wanted me to delete all the memories he had of his fiancée, who had left him at the altar. Initially I agreed to do the job. Daniel seemed excessively morose and I did think it was rather cruel of his beloved to not show up at the wedding after a year's engagement. He still had her wedding dress, he told me. He clung to it, and slept with it at night. That set off the first alarm bell, although I didn't pay it much attention. The other clues revealed themselves to me in viewing his recollection of the courtship, which got creepier and creepier the more I watched. There were hundreds of framed pictures of her, and them together as a couple, in his house. He used to check her phone while she was in the shower, and hold her still-warm clothes to his face and smell them for minutes at a time. He'd surprise her at work, and at drinks with her friends, and compulsively check to make sure she was wearing her engagement ring. He'd surreptitiously ruin the dresses of hers he didn't like, and buy her new ones that he approved of. He'd phone her often—too often—and expect her to jump to answer within a few rings every time, no matter where she was or what she was doing. If they argued, he would feign illness, and blame his mood on not feeling well, and she would cancel her plans in order to nurse him.

He used to watch her sleep. One night, he covertly snipped off a strand of her hair, tied a ribbon around it, and placed it in his secret drawer, along with the other small trophies he liked to collect.

Nothing he did was outright abuse, but his behaviour sent up so many red flags in my brain that I couldn't let him get away with it. I thought he must remember his disappointment with this girl —Anica, her name was, scribbled all over any scrap paper lying in the house—and perhaps he'd cool it with his next crush. Perhaps he would learn to not be so obsessive.

But I was wrong.

In the summer after refusing to take Daniel's case, Anica's body was found in a burnt-out car in Khayelitsha. It was set up like a hijacking gone wrong, and a local gang member was arrested, but I knew the truth. I took the data drive of Daniel's memory footage to the detective on the case and offered to project it on his wall, but he had more dead bodies on his hands than staff members, and it suited him to leave Anica's murder as open-

and-shut. When I lost my temper with him, telling him that Daniel would do it again, the detective eyed me suspiciously and told me I knew way too much about the couple's relationship, that it was *unnatural,* and touched the silver handcuffs on his belt. *Did I really want to be questioned?* he wanted to know. It was clear he meant as a suspect and not as an informer.

Anica's face still haunts me. She was so young, and so innocent-looking. I could have saved her life, but instead her body lies in ashes. Every now and then, when the guilt topples me, I go to see Daniel. I stalk him silently, hiding in the shadows. I look through his windows for pictures of new women. Once, I found him on a date with someone new, a pretty redhead, and I couldn't sleep for a week, imagining her hair being snipped off, her wrists bruised. Sometimes I still wake up to the scent of paraffin and a just-struck match.

Anica's black skeleton haunts me, but living people haunt me too.

I have all the stories here, in my library. Thousands of hours of backed-up memories.

Mostly I respect my clients' privacy enough to leave the footage alone. There is one exception, though.

I pour myself a whisky from one of the bottles Mr King was looking so longingly at, and dim the lights. I get comfortable on my favourite couch and close my eyes for a moment. I breathe deeply to settle my thoughts, and my heart. When I feel ready, I press play.

Memory footage of two young children appear on my cine-screen. They're playing in the back garden, chasing each other, laughing, screaming. They thrust their arms forward in Superman poses and jump off the edge of the raised vegetable beds. A dog comes into frame, a beautiful golden lab, and barks at the twin's excitement. I listen out for the woman's laugh: I know exactly where on the track it is. I've watched this—and her other deleted memories—a thousand times. Some of my favourites are of her looking in the mirror, so that I get to see her face. Those memories act as a booster to my own. I remember the feel of her skin, the scent of her hair. Sometimes I just get a glance, as she checks her eye makeup on her way out of the house. Sometimes it's luxuriously long, as she baths in front of the wide horizontal mirror in the bathroom. My mood starts to spiral, so I take a deep sip of my single malt and pull my thoughts back to the picture in front of me.

We're in the garden and the sun is shining.

She laughs again at the roughhousing of the kids, the excited dog, and then turns her head to look behind her, and that's when I see a younger version of myself. Scruffy hair; happy. Standing at the grill, turning some meat with silver tongs. I look up at her, and smile.

I always hate myself, then. Hate how smug I looked, how young and unscarred, and infuriatingly unaware of the danger in the world. I hate how I took it all for granted. Complained, even, about the messiness of the kids, the noise they made. Moaned about the broken nights of sleep and the crumbs on the floor. How golden it all looks now, in retrospect.

I sit in my neat, minimalist apartment, in the near-dark. There is no noise, and there are no crumbs on the floor. How quickly life changes. How much I wish I could go back in time and savour those lost moments.

What I do for a living now could be seen as a specialist branch of time travel. If only I had the technology to rewind real life. I turn off the screen and sit back into my chair, cradling my whisky glass in the dim light. I wonder how my wife is, what she's doing today. I feel the familiar urge to drive over to see her, but it's nothing more than a fantasy. She wouldn't recognise me. We used to love each other, madly and intensely, but she doesn't remember me anymore.

~

ACKNOWLEDGMENTS

Sincere thanks to:

My loyal fans. You have changed my life.

Mike, Keith & Gill for your love and your work.

Mom for always buying my books;

And to my generous Patreon supporters:

Joni Mielke
Elize van Heerden
Kriselda Gray
Claire Wickham
Kim Smith
Wendy Durison

ABOUT THE AUTHOR

JT Lawrence is an Amazon bestselling author,
playwright & bookdealer. She lives in Parkview, Johannesburg,
in a house with a red front door.

Be notified of giveaways & new releases by signing up to
JT's mailing list via Facebook or at

www.jt-lawrence.com

facebook.com/JanitaTLawrence

twitter.com/pulpbooks

bookbub.com/profile/jt-lawrence

Copyright © 2018 by JT Lawrence

All rights reserved.

No part of this book may be reproduced in any form or by any electronic or
mechanical means, including information storage and retrieval systems, without
written permission from the author, except for the use of brief quotations in a
book review.

❀ Created with Vellum

Made in the USA
Coppell, TX
20 August 2021

60863186R00127